W9-CUQ-472

Love is
a time of enchantment:
in it all days are fair and all fields
green. Youth is blest by it,
old age made benign:
the eyes of love see
roses blooming in December,
and sunshine through rain. Verily
is the time of true-love
a time of enchantment — and
Oh! how eager is woman
to be bewitched!

WHITE CAMELLIAS

Charlotte Gordon, a young and pretty American, had come to England to help her brother and his family during his hospitalization. Charlotte was delighted with Arden Manor and was very enthusiastic about the family drapery shop. Gradually, however, she became aware that a sinister threat was hanging over the shop, and that there was something more than routine carelessness involved in the disappearance of a bolt of cloth patterned in white camellias.

Books by Anne Tedlock Brooks
in the Ulverscroft Large Print Series:

ONE ENCHANTED SUMMER
FIRE IN THE WIND
ISLAND NEIGHBOR
SMOKE ON THE RIVER

ANNE TEDLOCK BROOKS

WHITE
CAMELLIAS

Complete and Unabridged

ULVERSCROFT
Leicester

First published in the
United States of America

First Large Print Edition
published July 1993

British Library CIP Data

Brooks, Anne Tedlock
  White camellias.—Large print ed.—
Ulverscroft large print series: romance
I. Title
813.54 [F]

ISBN 0–7089–2889–7

Published by
F. A. Thorpe (Publishing) Ltd.
Anstey, Leicestershire
Set by Words & Graphics Ltd.
Anstey, Leicestershire
Printed and bound in Great Britain by
T. J. Press (Padstow) Ltd., Padstow, Cornwall

This book is printed on acid-free paper

1

CHARLOTTE GORDON, walking down a garden path toward the ancient carriage house which had been converted into a modern garage, paused to pick a primrose. At the curve in the walk there was a great mass of them, violet blue, pressing against the mossy stones which had been set in place by the first owner of the manor.

Charlotte thought of that beautiful young woman. Her portrait, hanging over the mantel in Charlotte's room, lent vivid color to the otherwise staid surroundings. However, Charlotte's sister-in-law had done much to lift the quaint room from the doldrums by adding bright chintz drapes and spread. Now, at the end of her first week at Arden, Charlotte was rapidly falling in love with the place.

It was a crisp, clear April day. The sun had come out briefly, and promised to return. It was incredible that she had been in the bright California countryside just one week before, and that one of the jets had deposited her at London Airport only the previous Sunday.

"Come at once if you can, Charla. I know it's an imposition, but we need you like the very devil. Jennie has her hands full with the house and the kids, not to mention me," her brother, Barrett, had written. "I'll convalesce much better and quicker, knowing you're here and that your capable hands are helping run the shop."

So just two short weeks ago Charlotte had caught the pokey little cable car in San Francisco for the last time and had gone to talk it over with her boss. Mr. Clayton had seemed reluctant to let her go, she recalled with appreciation.

"Actually, Miss Gordon, a good secretary is hard to come by, and we'll miss you. But if your brother needs you, I'll give you six months leave, and we'll see how you like your work." He had added kindly, "You know, you may prefer to come back here even sooner, for business life isn't the same over there."

Yet actually, the tea time break was

2

much like the coffee break in the law firm. Jennie, her sister-in-law, had put in a plea for Charlotte, too. "You'll like the personnel in the shop, dear, and besides, Gordon really does need the lift you'll give him."

There hadn't been too much to keep Charlotte in San Fransisco, although her friendship with Greg Vincent had been moving along rapidly. I'm just a little glad to get away and see him from another perspective, she thought, as she walked on down to the garage. The little English car which her brother said she might use was polished and waiting.

"Wait a minute, Auntie Charla."

That was Judith, her brother's daughter. Judith was lean as a doe right now, but she had just emerged from pre-adolescent plumpness and sometimes still had a babyish look on her oval face.

"Can you stop at the pastry shop? Daddy wants some tarts."

"Yes, of course. Do you want to go with me?"

"I'd love to, but I'm helping polish silver right now. I've a tennis date this afternoon. I'd really rather go hiking with

3

you and Court, but Mums thinks I'd better play tennis with Jip. He's new, you know, and rather lonely."

Charlotte nodded. She touched Judith's shoulder briefly. "There'll be plenty of time this summer. We'll hike in the woods and up to the hilltop several times a week."

"Promise? People say they'll do things, but like Mums and Daddy, they just don't get around to it." A thirteen-year-old could suffer from loneliness and not say a word to anyone about it. It wasn't really cricket to complain to one's parents when they were unable to carry our promises.

Judith was wearing the blue jumper uniform of her private school. At home, at that age, Charlotte was thinking, she'd have been in Bermudas and tee shirt. One didn't loll on the grass at Arden Manor, if one's mother was the former Jennie Arden, great-great-granddaughter of the first Arden who had built the Manor house.

Charlotte started the car. "I'll see you in a couple of hours, honey." She waved at the straight little figure, with the real

4

gold hair which shimmered in the sun.

She drove down the lane, lined with huge tulip trees. The neat bordered box, freshly clipped and glossy green, gave the whole a neat, tidy look which it had not possessed even a week earlier.

"Things are a bit chaotic," Jennie had said last Sunday as they had driven out from the airport.

A bit of an understatement, Charlotte had thought as she first saw the untended lawns, the overgrown hedge and the unswept walks. But there was nothing wrong that some brawn and planning couldn't take care of. She suspected that in spite of help on the hospital bill and his government pension, her brother's recent operation had depleted his ready cash.

"Barrett's going to be a lot better, Charla, now that you're here to help things going a bit more smoothly. Actually, I like to have the children home at night, but I've been tempted to send them to boarding school. Judith's been attending St. Vincent's for three years, and a good day school is wonderful in many ways."

5

"Courtney's a big help," added Charlotte. "Barrett wrote me that he's taken on some of the yard work and that he's planning on a garden this summer."

"He's willing, but at eleven enthusiasm sometimes outmeasures energy. We've all been terribly hit, you know, by Barrett's losing his leg, Charla, but Court took it much harder than I'd thought he would. I found him out in the summerhouse last week, dissolved in tears. All I could get out of him was that his father couldn't play with the boys this summer. They've had a Little League Cricket Team the past two summers." Jennie paused. "Sometimes I think that's when Barrett's trouble started again. He slid on the wet grass and a week later had to go to the hospital. I don't think the old wound ever did really heal. We know the bone was involved."

Charlotte drove on toward the village of Kingston where she would be taking the daily bus to London, starting Monday.

The houses now were closer together. Ancient houses, set well back from the winding road, gave way to more modern dwellings with dooryards of flowers, some now in early bloom. By June great masses of color would fill every courtyard.

Charlotte had visited her brother in England twice since his marriage. He had been a young lieutenant in the army of occupation in Germany, and had met Jennifer in London when he visited an English officer soon after the war ended. Charlotte recalled how their parents had disliked the idea of his marrying an English girl, for he would probably spend the remainder of his life away from America.

Attending her brother's wedding fifteen years ago, Charlotte had been drawn to Jennifer and was easily able to see how her brother had fallen in love with her.

Jennifer had been living with an aged great-aunt who had died the following year. The big stone house needed all kinds of renovating and remodeling to make it habitable by Barrett's standards. It was two hundred years old and, as Charlotte's brother said, looked it!

Jennifer's father had died during the war, leaving her a draper's shop in London. It was in a sorry state until business picked up in the early 1950s. By that time Barrett had invested much of his inheritance and had sold some of Jennie's land. They had managed to live on in Arden Manor and to keep the shop going, although he had confessed to Charlotte he wondered if he had been wise.

"It would be much smarter to sell everything and go to America, I'm sure. But I simply can't tear Jennie away from tradition. I'm lucky she married me. And look at the kids. Judith is a replica of Jennie, and Courtney is the image of her father. I've never been able to infiltrate any American customs."

"I can see that," Charlotte said. After fifteen years, though Barrett had formerly preferred coffee, he had compromised with tea. The children attended private day schools, would even have had a nanny, as Jennie had had when a child, if there had been funds.

She couldn't picture either Barrett or herself atttending a private elementary school in California! But here it was the natural thing to do, quite expected.

She parked the little car with some

difficulty. It was different driving on the 'wrong' side of the street. Her bright blazer made a splash of color in the grayness of the street. A few people looked at her curiously, "That's the American sister of Jennier Arden," they seemed to be saying.

The village was small: the market, an ancient but rather small cathedral, a bakeshop, the pub, two book-shops, a confectioners, a chemist's shop and a few small key shops, tea rooms and hardware stores. Kingston was somewhat isolated, so there was a friendly feeling within the community, but one had to be born there or have relatives to be really accepted, Charlotte thought.

She did her shopping at the open market, loitering at the vegetables and selecting the poultry for tomorrow's dinner with some misgivings. A leg of lamb, some ducklings, some homemade sausages were on the list. She must get the tarts for her brother.

She had stopped by the key shop earlier in the week to have two keys made, one for the front door and one for a side door that hadn't been locked for years until her brother went to the hospital in Abingdale.

"Of course now we have the new man, but he has his own apartment above the old gate house, and I prefer it that way," explained Jennie, when they were speaking of the need for closing up the house more carefully than in the past.

There was the housekeeper and a younger upstairs maid who also served the evening meal. Molly, the older woman, was an able cook and had been with the family since she had been a girl. Her husband, the former gardener, had died last fall, and his nephew, a man of forty-five known as Mike Forrester, had taken his place. He hadn't been with them long enough for them to know much about him, although Courtney reported that he was a heavy tippler. Kit, the maid, was very quiet and not very well trained, according to Molly, but it was hard to find girls now who really put their hearts into their work.

As she drove back home, Charlotte wondered what she could do to help the situation at the house, which seemed to her to be rather disorganzied. Mike should have had the grounds in much better condition than she had found them. If he didn't improve and keep things up, she'd suggest they let him go and find another man.

She stalled the little car just beyond the last curve in the road, trying to avoid a tiny stream that had etched its way across the old paving. She flooded the engine and waited a few minutes before pressing the starter again. Suddenly she saw a horse and rider approaching. The man was young, dark-haired and straight in the saddle, the perfect picture of an Englishman taking his morning run.

He pulled up parallel to her on the bridle path, touching his hat. "Can I help you?"

"Thanks. I've just stalled the engine. It'll be all right in a minute."

"I'll wait a bit to make sure. Fine day."

"Beautiful day. And thanks for waiting. I'm not used to the car yet."

He patted the horse, got down from the saddle and walked over to the road. "I'm Jeff Carey, from down the road a bit, and I'll wager you're Barrett Gordon's sister."

11

"How do you do, Mr. Carey. Yes, I'm Charlotte Gordon."

"It's a pleasure to meet you. I've wondered when you'd arrive. Your brother told me you might come and help them out a bit, and he seemed very pleased."

"I don't know that I'll be much good in the shop, but it may relieve him to have someone around to look out for the family interests. Poor Jennie has her hands full."

"I'm fairly free on weekends, though I frequently have to go into London. Let me know if we can be of any help."

Charlotte thanked him, tried the starter once more and was successful. She glanced back at him and followed him through the rear view mirror almost unconsciously. Jennie would be pleased. She was worried that Charlotte would find small town life terribly dull after San Fransisco. "You must meet some of the younger people around," she had said, and had named Jefferson Carey and his sister Iris.

"They are our nearest neighbors. They were just youngsters when Barrett and I were married," Jennie had told her. "Jeff is handsome and has a good reputation as a barrister in London. Iris is away most of the winter in London for the social season. She's quite popular and brings lots of youngsters out to the house. Their parents were friends of my parents long ago. I hardly see them any more except at church and garden parties."

It was true that Barrett and she had not been able to keep up much of a social life. Barrett, injured during the last year of the war, had never really been too active, even before the old injury had flared up again.

It would be a long time before Barrett would be able to accept an artificial limb, although he was quite cheerful about it.

Now the large house with its grey stone walls and red roofs came into view. There was even a tower at the left, which completed the romantic picture she'd had of the place, Arden Manor, upon first hearing the name.

The evergreens were dark, the other trees were beginning to fill out, and some of the flowering shrubs were bright splashes against the landscape. A green meadow with two saddle horses, a few sheep and one cow attested to the fact that the place was still a gentleman farmer's home. A white post and rail fence with two stone columns divided the meadow from the landscaped grounds, and the sloping terrain rose gradually to the right until the eye following the outline of the trees reached the summit of a hill where family picnics had been held for two centuries. The hill fell off rapidly on the other side to the banks of the Thames. Here on summer days one could sit for hours and watch the small craft on the river.

It's really a lovely place, sighed Charlotte.

2

THE following Monday, Charlotte, accompanied by Jennifer, caught an early bus to London. It was fairly convenient transportation, as they could alight at the corner near the side street where Arden Drapers, Limited, had been situated for countless years. Everything in the long rows of city buildings, as far as the eye could see, seemed as ancient as the interior of the dim entry of the dark grey shop.

Charlotte felt a surge of excitement as they neared the busier sections and the bus was filled with early office commuters. Many of them had bought the *Times* and were reading, while others stared out of the windows. Some people looked dull; others glowed with anticipation. The quiet chatter of the London office girl was familiar, and now and then Charlotte caught a trace of cockney among the less fashionably clad.

On the whole, she thought, observing the quiet greys, navy blues and a few browns, the girls do not go in much for color in street clothes. She made a vivid splash in her crimson coat. I must really get a grey for commuting, she decided.

Jennie was looking better, although Charlotte knew that it had taken real effort for her to leave Barrett today. Judith was staying at home to look after her father, however, and was excited about making blueberry muffins for his tea.

"The next stop is ours," said Jennie. "Be sure to bring your umbrella."

The necessary evil, thought Charlotte. I must learn how to carry it so it looks like a walking stick. Really, Jennie looks so smart in her tweed suit. I'll never catch the hang of it all. I just look like a small town American girl, wholesome and vigorous. The job will be fun for the six months, anyway!

The bus slowed, stopped, and the girls descended. They walked quickly to the lobby of the building, Jennie giving a friendly nod to the bobby on the corner and smiling at the doorman. A light shower began just as they entered the swinging doors, and it seemed certain she'd need her umbrella, Charlotte thought as they went up in the lift.

The second floor was devoted to the offices and the shipping rooms of the company. Everything was clean, though badly in need of refreshing, lighter paint. It wasn't that the walls were dinghy, but simply dark to start with. Antiquity, antiquity! To be really good, does everything have to be old? Her own office back in San Francisco was in a modern building, all slick chrome and glass block and rubber tile, warm with color in the winter and cooled with an air conditioner in the summer.

"You must meet the employees first of all. Mr. Hugh Craigie is the manager now. Mr. Maleky is in charge of the larger divisions. It is a rather small shop, Charla, and I hope you won't be too disappointed. The girls are not very special, so you may not want to get too close. Of course you'll go out for tea and lunch with them, but they're not really your kind, dear."

17

Some of the old caste system is still working, Charla thought, squeezing her sister-in-law's arm. "Don't worry honey; I'll take care not to break through that little wall. They won't accept me, anyway. I've had a little chance to observe how this works."

Marty Adamson, the girl who worked in the retail shop, and Bonnie Brewer seemed like the familiar picture she'd drawn mentally of girls who worked in drapers' shops.

There was a decorator, Miss Tomlinson, who probably still believed in anti-macassars, and who greeted Jennie with courtesy and gave a still little nod to Charlotte. "I hope you'll like it here, although we're not as modern as some," she said in a clipped voice.

The whole place had a well-bred look. The carpeting was dark green, sprinkled with small red roses, the high windows were shuttered with circumspect mahogany, and the cases and tables were immaculate and neatly laid out with fabrics.

The Liberty silks, on which their reputation chiefly rested, were truly beautiful, Charlotte thought wistfully, as Jennie exclaimed over the beautiful new designs. "You'll have fun here, if you have a chance to come in once in a while."

"I'm not really sure what my job is," murmured Charlotte. The older man, Maleky, was approaching.

"Oh, I think you're to meet the public, act as secretary or work in the retail shop. We'll ask Mr. Maleky."

He was a kindly old gentleman. He had been with the firm for forty years, beginning as an errand boy for Jennie's grandfather.

"I'm sure that we can find a spot for you to help us out," he said to Charlotte. "Your brother and I had a little talk about you just last week. I think the best way for you to break in is to help a little in the retail shop, because we need someone right now. One of the girls is ill at home, leaving us short-handed. There really is not very much pressure. People must make up their minds on upholstery and drapery."

"Yes, some live with their choices the remainder of their lives." Jennie moved restlessly. "Has Mr. Craigie come in yet?"

"No. He's a bit late this morning. Was off on holiday and will not get in till eleven, Mrs. Gordon. May I help you?"

"I want to introduce my sister-in-law all around, but I have a bit of shopping to do and can come back. We might go out for tea presently, Charla."

"That'll be lovely. I'll just put my things away and do a few things to Barrett's desk. He asked me to get some papers out of his files."

"I'll help her," offered Maleky. "I'll see she meets Mr. Craigie, if he comes in before you get back."

Jennie left the shop, and Charlotte was whisked off to her brother's office, locked since his absence.

The office was rather larger than she'd expected, roomy and dignified, with dark, heavy furnishings, leather chairs, a Persian rug on the floor, a fireplace with white tiles and marble mantel. A good etching above it and several hunting prints and pictures of birds must have pleased her brother, for she could see that they had been there for some time, and he was a little impatient with pictures unless he liked them.

She felt lost in the big leather chair facing the desk, and after Mr. Maleky had gone she opened the files tentatively. There was an Italian account that Barrett wanted to see about. She opened the folder and noted the last date. It had been inactive since the preceding summer. Barrett wanted to try and find out why.

"I'm feeling frustrated, Sis, but I can direct a few activities from my wheel chair. I got to thinking of a few things while I was in the hospital, wondering why we couldn't move things out a little faster, have a larger volume of business."

"Bigger and better business! That's the American philosophy, of course. I'll be glad to do everything possible."

"You're been in a spot in your office where you can see how business is handled. Maleky is getting old, and I'm not so sure that we can afford to keep him on many more years. We need someone in his place to get going."

"I'm not your man, but I'll help!"

There was a folder for a Fleet Street address which Barrett was also interested in seeing. She riffled through it with interest. Two dozen bolts of sheeting, fourteen bolts of chintz, muslin, special highland tweed, some Shetland Island knitted yardage, hand-loomed. A good healthy account, I should think, murmured Charlotte to herself. It may be small potatoes, though, to a firm such as this.

Is Arden Limited as small as I'd been led to believe? she wondered.

Mr. Craigie had come in now, she noticed as she left her brother's office with the folders under her arm. She would put them with her coat and umbrella, so she would remember them.

Maleky brought the younger man toward her and introduced them. Hugh Craigie was about forty or so, a thin, rather nervous man, with a small clipped mustache, dark eyes and hair. He was rather pale, it seemed to Charlotte, and she wondered if he might be feeling ill.

He was most gracious with her and asked her to go out with him for tea. "We want you to feel comfortable,

Miss Gordon, and get acquainted. Your brother was most fortunate that you were willing to come and help him out."

As Charlotte thanked him for the invitation and explained why she wouldn't be able to go, she wondered at his effusive greeting, and felt it was overdone. Everyone else had been quietly pleasant, and she hadn't expected this cordiality. Jennie came back while Marty was showing her around the retail shop, explaining the rows of small cabinets and their contents.

"There's a ducky little tea room over about two streets; I want you to see it. They make the most divine pastry. I only have it when I come in with Barrett, about twice a year," Jennie said as they went down in the lift. "Up one flight, and it's worth every step. Besides, some of my friends drop in occasionally. I want you to meet anyone who might be there."

The room was warm and filled with the smell of good coffee and spices; and the hot cross buns were just being brought in.

"I know you like good coffee. I can get

tea, here, too, and there's nothing like the old brass and the hearth in this place."

"It's quite inviting." Charla felt at once that this would be her own little shop, too, for tea and maybe lunch.

Luckily, one of Jennie's friends did appear, an older, white-haired woman with a little girl in tow.

"My dear, I heard about your husband. I'm so sorry; we're hoping everything will turn out well. Is he better now?"

Jennie nodded. "It takes time, but it'll be better for him once we all get used to the idea. This is his sister from America. Charla, one of my mother's best friends, Mrs. Cavendish. And this must be little Rosemary."

Her granddaughter was spending a fortnight with Mrs. Cavendish, who had brought her in to buy a riding outfit and to go to a gallery.

Charla, absorbing as much of the quiet talk as possible, began to feel more relaxed and thought the shop might almost be a coffee shop back home.

They were there almost an hour, which was really quite a coffee break by American standards. "Shouldn't I be getting back to the shop?" whispered Charlotte. "I'm a working girl, you know."

"Not this first day!" smiled Jennie.

But they were soon out on the walk returning to the shop, where Jennie left her so she could take an early bus back to Kingston where they'd left the car. "I'll meet you at six sharp," said Jennie.

"I won't miss the bus. I can't, you know; it's so convenient. And thanks, Jennie, for helping me get acquainted. If I need any help around the shop, I feel that Mr. Maleky is my friend. And Marty looks like a good soul, if she'd only stop acting like a frightened rabbit."

"So many of the girls have queer ideas about your American ways. They'll think, because you dress well and have a watch, some jewelry and are Barrett's sister, you are probably quite rich. And of course they read the American magazines and know all about the sophisticated working girl. Don't let it bother you, but you're in for a thorough scutiny!"

Charlotte laughed. "I'll mind my p's and q's, then!"

The afternoon was a little wearing. She

25

did go to lunch with Mr. Craigie, about one o'clock, and they didn't get back to the shop until almost three. The girls were a little busy and she felt guilty.

She didn't quite know what to make of Mr. Craigie. He was very businesslike, and they discussed what she would do in the shop. He ordered a very good lunch, and she knew that she'd not be able to eat this way often or she'd have a weight problem. He was thoughtful and courteous, and she appreciated some of the things he told her about the business.

The thing that startled her the most was that she later saw him going through the folders that she had laid out to take home to her brother. The idea came to her that if Barrett had wanted to take care of the problems, he would have had only to telephone Craigie from his home.

3

JENNIE was waiting at the bus stop for her when Charlotte alighted, and thus began the first week in her new job. They drove back to Arden slowly, exchanging the news of the afternoon.

"Barrett is so anxious to see you and to get your opinion on how things are going," Jennie told her.

"It's too early," said Charlotte. "I can't really tell much about it from my quick overall view today. I didn't meet the accountant, and the shopping clerks were too busy to be interrupted. I had no idea that the business was that large."

"Oh, we do a fairly good volume, but it's not nearly as large as when my father ran the place. In fact," Jennie sighed ruefully, "my great-grandfather would laugh at this little company. He used to occupy most of the big building, and as you saw, we now have only the second floor and two offices on the first. It's enough, though. All we need is just to pay the upkeep, and to go along as we are. The house is badly in need of repair in spots, but nothing pressing."

Making light of the situation, Charlotte smiled. "Is Judith home yet? I promised to go for a walk with her this evening after dinner. We'll make it a quick, short one."

"Don't let her impose on you. Barrett will want to talk with you, but don't let him at the dinner table."

"I promise!"

Mike was raking up dead leaves around the hedge of lilacs, and the tulips were looking as though ready to burst into bloom. Jennie deftly turned into the narrow winding drive and parked the car in the garage.

Courtney and Judith burst from the back door of the house.

"Hello! How was the first day?" the boy greeted Charlotte.

"Did you have lunch with Mr. Craigie? Isn't he the spiffy one?" Judith asked.

Charlotte laughed. "The first day was fine. And I did have lunch with Mr. Craigie. A two-hour lunch, such as we don't dare take back in California.

We're lucky to have forty minutes and a sandwich at the nearest snack bar."

"And a malted?"

"Not always. Have to watch the figure!"

"You're just right," sighed Judith. "Last year I was abominably fat and had to cut out pastry and cream."

"Some hardship, too, for her," said Court.

"You should talk!"

"Let's go say hello to your Daddy," suggested Charlotte. "I'm sure he's anxious to see if I got his folders home."

"Wish he wouldn't worry about the office," sighed Jennie.

Barrett was up in the wheel chair. Mike had come in from work about four and helped him into it. Charlotte thought Barrett looked a bit better today. There seemed to be a little more color in his cheeks and his eyes looked brighter. His hair shone greyer in the light of the table lamp; his hands were thin, and the veins were pale blue streaks across the white skin. He was combed and shaved and wore a fresh white sports shirt. He smiled at his sister as she entered.

"Pretty grim?"

"Not at all, Barrett. You know how it is the first week in any new place. Exciting and a little uncertain, while you wonder how the staff will accept you."

"No worry there. Maleky is just like Gibralter, and has been adjusting himself to all kinds of changes for forty years. How did you find Craigie?"

"Right in there pitching. Gave me a hearty though dignified welcome, key to the city and all that kind of thing. Couldn't have been more pleasant." Let's just pass up the fact that you thought he was too effusive, Charlotte thought. "I was shown the rounds by the girls, and of course by Mr. Maleky, and given lunch by your man, Craigie."

She handed him the folders. "I think these are what you want. Why don't you look over them, and I'll get ready for dinner? But no shop talk at the table, remember."

He nodded in agreement. "It's deadly, all right. I'll see you before bedtime here. I understand you have promised Judy a walk." He opened a folder. "Don't let the kids impose on you."

"I won't. But I love to be with them. Maybe Court will go along, too."

"Wouldn't count on it. He's hunting specimens for his science laboratory."

Climbing the winding stairs to her room on the second floor, Charlotte wondered how many hundreds of people had climbed these same steps. Some of them watched her from their portraits, which were lined up in gallery style at the top of the stair well.

There was the great-great-grandmother, Judith, and the great-grandmother, Jennifer, each charming in her own way. There was a resemblance between the first one and Jennie, Barrett's wife. Heavy gold frames detracted from rather than enhanced the features, and Jennifer's green ballgown was a little familiar, in spite of its years. She was a vivid, spirited girl, one could see, with coal black hair and disdainful lips.

Charlotte's eyes sought and found that first Jennifer's father. With a roman nose, piercing blue eyes, dark hair streaked with grey, an imperial look on his handsome face, he was a Courtney. That was why Barrett's son was named Courtney, of course. His great-great-grandfather had been disinherited by the Earl of Courtright; perhaps that was why he wore a haughty expression. Maybe he had had a right to, for he had been able to build a larger house, Courtney Hall, had had more servants, more silver and more social prestige than his own father. And of course he had passed that fortune on to his daughter who had married an Arden.

It's all too much for me, Charlotte thought a little guiltily. Ancestors!

She went down the long hallway to her own room. High-ceilinged and lightened by the new blue chintzes which Jennie had used on the bed and windows, it was really not too bad. The French bedroom suite, white and gold, heavily ornate, was also made more cheerful by modern accessories.

It was colder outdoors now, and someone, Kit probably, had lit the fire. It was burning brightly, and Charlotte stood before it gratefully.

There was the double photograph of her own parents which she always carried with her on long trips. She picked it up from the long dressing table and smiled into their eyes. It had taken her years to accept their death in an air crash. But she could look at them now without a rush of tears and the old empty feeling. She and her brother had lived with their grandmother in a big house on Russian Hill for years, until he enlisted. Her grandmother had died two years ago. Barrett and his family were the only family she had now. Charlotte felt a little tired tonight, but still she was very grateful for the feeling of security that her brother and his family gave her.

Dinner was ready when she went downstairs, Jennie had caught Judith's hand just as she had raised it to strike the ancient gong in the lower hall.

Charlotte giggled as she realized the suppression was for her own sake. She recalled the temple bells from India that her grandmother had had hanging in her hall, and with what delight Charlotte used to clang them.

Mike was wheeling in her brother's chair very slowly, and Courtney very quietly followed them. Tonight Judith was wearing the pedal pushers and bright tee shirt which Charlotte had brought her from California. She looks just like an American teen-ager, Charlotte thought.

There was an excellent roast beef and Yorkshire pudding, spring greens and boiled potatoes and caesar salad. Court was especially fond of it, Jennie explained.

"I think it's because his daddy makes the dressing, and because of the great ceremony with which he mixes the salad at the table. We have to serve it at least twice a week."

"You did a beautiful job polishing the silver Saturday," Charlotte said to Judith as they began the meal.

"I like to. I think in America I would major in home economics."

"And why not here?"

"Oh, here one studies languages and the piano. Boys take law or medicine."

One couldn't say, "Oh, nonsense!" The kids must have a lot of conflicts, with an American father and an English mother.

Molly, the cook-housekeeper had prepared a delicious dessert, a sort of custard cream with strawberries served in small dishes. Kit was not as good at serving meals as the first maid who had formerly worked there. Barrett liked good service, and it did seem strange that Jennie had continued to let Kit work for them.

Charlotte overlooked the spot that a slight jostle of Kit's hand had caused as she lowered the dessert in front of her, but Judith said something in a low tone to her mother as Kit went back into the kitchen.

Jennie flushed. "I'm sorry, Charla. Kit isn't very good. She really isn't very good at cleaning, either. I'll try to replace her soon. I'd never have taken her, if we'd not been so desperate at the time."

"Don't worry, Jennie. It's all right."

But it was the small details that made Jennie nervous, Charlotte could see, so perhaps in the long run it would be wise to replace Kit.

As soon as the meal ended, the two children and Charlotte went for their walk. It was past twilight and would soon be dark, so they stepped out with speed along the wide path, avoiding the woods where, Judith admitted, she used to think gnomes and druids hid in the daytime and came out to dance by the light of the moon at night.

"Is the old stone stile just beyond the little meadow?" asked Charlotte, recalling suddenly the charm on the marker between the grounds of Arden Manor and the Carey estate.

"Oh, yes! We'll take a look at it. I used to crawl over the steps when I was learning to walk, if Daddy would put me down. I bumped my nose on it several times," said Courtney.

"Look! There goes Jeff Carey on his big horse!" cried Judith. "Haloo, Jeff! Haloo, Jeff!"

The man turned and waved at them. He guided his horse toward them, over the meadow adjoining the Arden meadow. "Don't let him spoil our walk now," admonished Judith.

"You're the one who had to go and call to him!" said Court.

4

WHILE Charlotte and Jeff Carey chatted a few minutes, the children played a game of tag, in and out of the native shrubs and trees. Their cries and laughter became more and more distant, until presently Charlotte said that she would have to go.

"I've a message to give to you. My parents would like you to come to dinner one evening soon. How about Thursday evening?" Jeff asked.

"Thank you. That is very nice of them."

"They'll be delighted. I'll pick you up about eight."

She nodded and smiled. "That'll be just right. This commuting is going to take a little doing until I'm used to it."

"It's not bad, really. Gives one a chance to sort out plans for the day." He touched his hat. "I'll see you Thursday."

He rode off on his beautiful horse.

Court and Judith raced back to her, and they walked as far as the stile, then turned back in the dusk. There would be an early moon, a full, bright one.

They could see Mike with a flashlight coming from the stables, and they heard one of the cows lowing for its new calf. They talked a little about plans for the weekend and about the examinations which would be coming up soon at school.

The kitchen area was dark and quiet, and there was a small light in the servants' wing.

"Kit's going to the cinema with Mike tonight," volunteered Court.

"I don't think Mum will like that, either," said Judith. "She isn't quite sure of Mike yet. And I don't think she wants Kit to associate with him."

Charlotte quickly changed the subject, and then they were at the little-used side doors and scraping off the soles of their shoes before entering.

"Better go get your baths, sprouts, and I'll see you at breakfast." She kissed Judith's forehead and touched Court's shoulder.

"We're so glad you came," said Judith. "Things will be a lot better now."

"I'm glad too, honey."

She was just ready to turn the night lock on the door when she heard Mike's low whistle and saw Kit darting from the side door of the servants' wing. Then Mike's old car started up and they were gone for the evening. It was not really her affair, Charlotte thought as she went down the hall to her brother's study. He was sitting chatting with Jennie, who was doing some needlework.

"Sit here, Charla. I'll tuck the kids in, and they needn't say good night this evening. I know that you'll have a lot to talk about." Jennie gathered up her work and put it away in her basket. "I'll come back in about an hour, dear."

"Right," said Barrett. "Cigarette, Sis?" He held out the silver case she had sent him for Christmas. "I forgot. You've never gotten the habit, have you?"

"I don't really like them. Shall I build up the fire?"

"Not now, unless you're chilly. Did you have a good walk?"

"Yes, and I plan to do a lot of walking.

Incidentally, we ran into Jeff Carey on his horse. I have a dinner invitation for Thursday evening, at Carey Hall."

"Good! Jennie will be happy about it. You'll like the Careys. They've been wonderful to Jennie all through the years." He picked up one of the folders she had brought from his office. "Now, this account — " he began.

An hour later when Jennie came back into the room, he was still talking about information from the folders.

"That's positively all for tonight," commanded his wife.

"Just one more thing, Charla."

"She'll be worn out, and on the very first day, too!"

"Quiet, woman," grinned Barrett.

Presently Charla found herself going upstairs to her room. "Seven o'clock comes fairly early in England, I've noticed, just the same as in San Francisco." Even then I'll have to dash to catch the eight o'clock bus, she thought.

To save time Kit would bring her tray up every morning at seven-twenty, and Charla would be ready to go to the station at seven-forty. This week Mike would be driving her there and meeting her in the evening, but she saw no reason she shouldn't bicycle the four miles as soon as the weather permitted. It would be wonderful exercise.

She took a warm bath, brushed her hair and wrote two letters. One was a long delayed one to her friend, Greg Vincent. He would wonder why she hadn't written him sooner as she'd promised at the airport when he'd taken her to catch the polar flight for London.

Now Greg seemed very far away, a dim figure in a strangely distant past.

The second day at the shop was a bit more interesting. She began to understand the confusing procedures. The sales slips were different from those she had used one summer when she had worked in a department store at home. The money exchange was becoming familiar, though guineas and pounds and half-crowns demanded full attention.

She didn't go out for tea. Presently one of the girls called to her, "Wouldn't you like a cup of tea, miss? We all have tea about this time."

"Yes, thank you."

"Come on with me. We meet in this little room back here, where there's a plate and a pot, and we take turns bringing the cakes."

"Sounds nice and cozy."

"It's warming. Most of us get up early, and there's not much time," said Bonnie Brewer. She looked as though she needed more time for her office grooming. Her skirt was fairly new, but the sweater she was wearing had seen better days and was worn thin in spots. Her blonde hair was strained tightly at the temples and combed back to form a bun at the nape of her neck. If her eyes had had proper arches above, instead of scraggly brows, she'd have been more attractive, and a bit of rouge would have brightened the blue.

Marty was plump, on the good-natured side, and a wee bit inquisitive, just as Jennie had told Charlotte. The 'frightened rabbit' of yesterday was entirely gone today. Perhaps she had been awed by the presence of the boss' wife.

After tea, Charlotte realized they'd been able to get quite a bit of information from her. She had six months' leave, she was staying with her brother's family, she thought she'd enjoy her work at the shop, and she had been a secretary back home.

Mr. Craigie seemed very busy today. There were a number of calls for him, and Charla was given the task of answering his phone. His secretary was home ill, and by early afternoon he called Charla into his office and asked her to take over until the regular girl returned.

"Can you take dictation, Miss Gordon?"

"Yes. And I use the dictaphone, too."

"Good. We must think of equipping the office with one or two later. I've some letters to get out by evening. Will you write them for me?"

Thus within one day she became substitute secretary, with only a rueful glance or two at the beautiful fabrics she had hoped to work with for a while at least.

To her surprise, one of the letters dictated was to go to the Italian firm which her brother had discussed with her the previous night. It seemed to be an excellent letter. Her brother had planned on sending this type of promotion to them, so she believed he would be pleased to see that Craigie was looking after it. She'd remember to mention it tonight.

Lunch was just a sandwich and a cup of coffee at a small dining room across from the building housing Arden, Limited. She recalled the elaborate luncheon of yesterday as she ate, and thought, I'm just one of the employees today, which suits me fine! She had never made a point of having coffee in the afternoon and didn't join the girls at tea at three-thirty. They made quite a ritual of it; she noticed that at least thirty minutes were consumed. Of course Bonnie had a long bus ride and seldom reached home before six-thirty in the evening. She lived with her mother and six children in an overcrowded flat.

Sometimes, Bonnie said, she stayed in London with friends. "And it's a bit of all right, too; makes me feel like I'm on holiday! You don't know what it's like, miss, not having a life of your own. My Mums likes her beer, and she's always having in her gentlemen, and so I like to get away now and then."

44

Marty said, "Why don't you stay in London, Bonnie? You could find a roommate."

"No, I couldn't. I promised my papa."

By the end of the fourth day Charlotte knew very little about Marty, although they continued to have tea.

Jennie admonished Charla about it. "They'll take you for granted in a month. Be a good girl and go to the tea room around the corner. You'll soon meet some other girls and maybe a young man or two, although I wouldn't encourage that."

"I'll be most circumspect," laughed Charla.

Mrs. Cavendish called her at the office the very next morning, and Charla was certain her sister-in-law had promoted the invitation to tea. She couldn't get away, but promised to accept the next time.

The day seemed interminably long, for that was the evening she was to have dinner with the Careys. She took an early bus, having promised Jennie that she'd get to Kingston in time to rest a bit and spend a leisurely hour getting ready before Jeff called for her.

It was a lovely afternoon and the rush was not yet on at the station. Jennie was waiting, and they had a cup of tea at the inn before driving on to Arden Manor. Relaxed and anticipating a pleasant evening, Charlotte looked prettier than she had since her arrival. A little above average height, she wore her tweed suit with an air. Her shoes and bag matched perfectly, and her pert hat rested prettily on her dark hair.

Her brother eyed her with approval when she reached the house. "Hey! You look pretty well after four days in a new job. What do you think, Jennie?"

"I agree. Maybe it's the plans for the evening. Mrs. Carey called me this afternoon, and they're looking forward to meeting you, Charla."

"I think Jeff was impressed. And that's something!" added Barrett. "He's had the pick of the girls around here, you know. Meets quite a few through that sister of his in London, too."

"Iris is so different from Jeff. She's much more socially inclined, like her mother. Jeff and his father are more alike, quiet and reserved, with a love for the land."

"You have to do more than farm nowadays, though. Jeff's a well known barrister."

"But I can see him thirty years from now, retired, perhaps serving in Parliament, the legendary English squire."

Jennie and Barrett smiled. "Perhaps," said Jennie. "By the way, his mother wants to send over a horse for you. Said he needs the exercise and it would be a favor."

"I've not ridden for years, and then not very well," said Charla. She brightened. "I'd like to try again, though. Think young Court and Judith would like to join me occasionally?"

"Of course!" cried Barrett. "And Jennie, too. She's a keen horsewoman, but hasn't had any chance recently."

"Very well. I'll agree, then — as a favor to the Careys' horse, of course." Charlotte's blue eyes twinkled.

She hummed a little as she went upstairs to bathe and change for the evening. She took her time, pouring in fragrant bath salts, and enjoying the

47

warm water and the rest of the grooming ritual. She selected a new blue silk dress, certain that Jeff would like it, and smiled to herself when she realized that she was deliberately hoping he would. The dress was full-skirted and had a lovely neckline. She omitted the brilliant necklace she sometimes wore, but added a pair of pearl earrings and a tiered pearl bracelet. Simple and elegant, she thought, critically viewing herself in the full length mirror on the dressing room door.

A few mintues later she heard the sound of wheels on the drive and picked up her small purse and a fresh lace-edged handkerchief. She paused and touched her temples with her favorite perfume.

It had been some time since she had felt this excited about a date, she suddenly realized. Greg and San Francisco seemed very far away.

5

THE Carey estate lay off the main road to Kingston, about three miles down a small country road. At the rise of the hill Charlotte could see the large greystone house with its two long wings, its red roofs and the surrounding buildings which housed tenant farmers and employees. She had expected a more lavish place than Arden Manor, but was not prepared for the great house and its forest and fields.

"Mother is hoping that Iris will get here in time for dinner. She tried to reach her yesterday, but found her off on a trip with friends and hasn't been in touch with her yet. She left a message, but I'm not sure if she'll be here tonight."

"I'm eager to meet her. Jennie and my brother have mentioned her several times."

"We always knew where Iris was when she disappeared for hours when she was growing up. She could always be found over at Arden Manor. She had quite a crush on Jennie and then later on your brother, Barrett."

"They're very fond of her."

Jeff smiled at her. He was impeccable in his dark blue suit, tailored perfectly. His grey hat was pulled slightly over his brow; his blue eyes were deep-set and black-lashed.

He drove up the winding drive slowly, and she noted the clipped hedge, the brilliant colors of late tupils and the fragrance of flowering trees. The grass was cropped short along the fence rows and she saw several small lambs frolicking about the sheep in the meadows. The stables were white, the paddocks some distance from the house. A shining convertible, an American make, was under the sheltering porte-cochere.

"Iris did get home!" Jeff said, delight in his tone.

He parked in the curve of the drive and helped Charlotte from the car.

He opened the heavy door of the house, and they stepped into a well-lighted hall. The sun was down now, but a bit of rosy light came through a western, diamond-shaped window, lighting up the interior of the vast room to which Jeff led Charla.

"Here we are, Father," said Jeff.

A tall, spare man rose, laying aside his newspaper, and came forward, hand extended.

"Miss Gordon, may I present my father?"

The older man smiled at her, and Charla noted the strong resemblance between father and son.

Mrs. Carey came in just at that moment, and Charla was caught up by the warmth of her smile and her pleasant manner. "We're so happy to have you. And our daughter Iris just drove in, too. She'll be delighted."

Mrs. Carey and Charlotte sat on the long divan while the men chose deep chairs beside the fireplace. A few logs burned low, putting a rich glow on the patina of the old paneling and the dark furniture. A few good paintings hanging on the soft grey walls impressed Charlotte. She recognized one of them as a famous original which she would have expected to find in the National Gallery.

Yet it seemed right that some of the lesser known landscapes and portraits of the old masters should be there.

Mrs. Carey spoke of an approaching annual garden party. "We always have one late in May or early in June depending on the weather."

Charlotte had to come, of course, and Jennie and Judith. "It's too much to hope your brother may come out this soon?"

Charlotte shook her head. "Not for many weeks yet, I'm afraid. He doesn't even seem restless yet. I've been afraid that he'd be unwilling to stay in so long, but he seems unwilling to do more than go from his room to the dining table. A little later, perhaps, we'll get him outdoors to the porches."

Iris, who came downstairs just before the maid announced dinner, was more charming than Charla had expected. She was very pretty, wearing her softly waved blonde hair in the new 'beehive' fashion, which was quite fetching on her. Her green dinner dress was of soft rippling silk, very short, almost sleeveless, and with a deep V neckline. Her color was rather high, her hazel eyes flashing. Her conversation was exuberant, and Charla was almost certain that she'd already had more than one cocktail.

"How absolutely wonderful that you could come over while Jennie and Barrett need you so," she said presently, after explaining to her parents why she'd been unable to call them the night before. "Those little ducks of theirs, Court and Judith, how are they?"

The butler served drinks, and Charla took a sip or two just to be sociable. She had never really cared for cocktails, and saw no reason to pretend.

"You'll not believe it, I'm sure, Mums, but I saw Tony and Meg yesterday. It was in a little shop not far from Harrod's. I'd gone into that leather place to get the strap fixed on my camera. There they were, as big as life."

"And is she as pretty as claimed?" asked Charla.

"Much prettier! I've seen her many times over the years, but hardly at all recently."

"Dinner is served," announced the butler from the arched doorway.

Jeff escorted Charla and Iris. The

dining room was more formal than the large drawing room. Family portraits graced the dark walls, and Charla, letting her eyes rove over them, recognized familiar features repeated in the present members of the family.

Dinner was rather long and a bit tedious, according to American standards. Elaborately, with the help of a maid, the butler passed the food deftly, serving it as though his very life depended upon formality.

Iris, now a bit subdued, addressed a question or two to Charla, and plied her brother with them. Jeff answered her with restraint.

She pouted a little. "But it's a phenomenal case. What do you think they'll do with the defendant if they find him guilty?"

"Iris! Now let's change the subject. The papers are full of it, and your brother can't tell you any more," admonished her mother.

"Might as well ask Jerry Nichols on the *Times*. He'd probably tell me more."

Jeff laughed. "An excellent source. Maybe he can give me a tip, too. Are you going to the races next week?"

Neat, thought Charla. Then Iris was off on a discussion about the upcoming races at Lingfield Park, Surrey. She planned to attend an open tennis tournament at Beckenham, Kent, and on Friday of the following week the All-England L.T.C., Wimbledon, for the Women's International Championship Wightman Cup Match.

"We don't make any attempt to keep up with Iris and her interest in sports these days," murmured Mrs. Carey. "But if you like horse shows, the one at Richmond, Surrey, the Royal Show, is exceptional. We'd be pleased to have you in our party."

"I can go on a Saturday, but I want to stay pretty close to Arden Manor for the first two weeks or so," Charla answered.

"Later, then," nodded the older woman.

As they returned to the drawing room, Jeff, walking beside Charla, cupped her arm in his hand. "I'd planned on taking you around a bit, Miss Gordon, if you'd like. There's always tennis, there's polo, and of course the plays."

"Give me a little more time. Soon I should be able to do almost any of the galleries, and I do like racing."

"How about ballet? *Harlequin in April* is at Sadler's Wells."

She nodded. The summer began to look brighter. The prospects of having Jeff for an escort excited Charlotte. She wondered if he had no serious feelings about any other girl.

She stole a glance at him as they chatted a few minutes with his parents. He was probably nearing the age of thirty. At least in America she knew that young, successful lawyers were usually about twenty-four before they earned their law degrees and passed the bar examinations. He surely must have been out in the field for at least five years to have gained prestige. Later she was surprised to learn that he had gone to Oxford at an early age and was now only twenty-seven.

"Why don't you turn on the flood lights and show Miss Gordon the gardens?" suggested his mother. "There's no dew yet, but you'll need your stole, my dear."

Iris had gone into the study to turn on her new hi-fi set, and the strains of the *Flower Drum Song* wafted gently from the open window as they walked down the paved garden path. The full moon shone and the air was filled with little whisperings of a heady spring, with night rustlings and the chirping of a tree frog. Crickets sang along the path and there was a gentle splash from the fountain where the water sparkled in the shaft of light.

She shivered.

"Too cool for you? I forget how warm it must be back in your home country. I always thought I'd like to see California. I've been to New York twice, but always on business; a flight over, two or three days at your incredible American pace, and then back to London."

"It is a little cool," she said in a low voice.

She was thinking about the incredible things she'd found in England! A bit defensively she recalled the run-down condition of her brother's shop. In New York, the whole place would have been as busy as a beehive; none of that two-hour-for-lunch, forty-minutes-for-tea stuff! And you'd know just where you stood as far as finances were concerned. She suddenly wondered why Jennie and Barrett were not more informed concerning the shop. A few things had come up just this week that made her feel impatient. It did seem as though they were about fifty years behind the times.

Mr. Maleky was stilted and nineteenth-centuryish, and it occurred to her suddenly that Craigie was not much more modern. But then, maybe it was the tradition of the place which kept them going. She had begun to see that the accounts of many of their customers were in arrears, and that letters explaining delays were as old-fashioned as the shop in which the business was being conducted.

Streamline production! They ought to go en masse to Dearborn and see the Ford plants! Charla thought suddenly, and almost laughed aloud at the ludicrous idea.

Jeff was guiding her toward the house now, and she said, "I think it's getting late. I catch an early bus, you know."

"Yes, I just realized that you must be commuting every day. Would you like to ride into London occasionally with me? Or better yet, I could pick you up once in a while in the evening and bring you out to Arden."

"That would be very nice. But only when it's convenient."

"Yes, of course. Sometimes I spend half a day at our local office or over at Adingdale. On short notice, too, so it's better for me just to call you."

"Sounds fine," Charla said. "Now I'll just say good night to your parents and sister."

Iris came in to add her invitation to Charla to return soon, and suggested they have lunch in the city sometime in the next week or so. "I've a duck of a little apartment at Grosvenor House, and should you wish to stay over with me sometime, give me a ring. I'm usually in town two or three days a week."

"She legitimizes it by taking painting lessons," her mother said affectionately. "And of course, it does make a nice place for me to drop in when I'm worn out from shopping."

"Mostly it's to be able to get away from the dullness of country life," stated Iris frankly. "It can be deadly here in the winter, watching the rain stream from the skies."

"It's not that bad, Iris!" protested Jeff. "You'll frighten away Miss Gordon."

"Not a little rain!"

It was later than she'd realized, Charla found as she turned out the night light left for her before going upstairs at Arden.

6

BY the end of the third week at Arden, Limited, Charlotte had found her own little niche. She seemd to fit into the pattern of the established routine at the shop fairly well. The secretary she was substituting for had sent in her resignation, saying that she was going to be married in June and preferred to take her leave now.

So it seemed natural for Charlotte to remain in the post first given her, rather than be an all-round employee. In some ways it pleased her better to have a definite job and to be able to plan her work each day. It also gave her a good reason for being unable to take tea with the other girls in the shop without offending them.

"Ducky, you can always come out and make yourself a cup of tea any time you wish," Bonnie said one day. "It's too bad you can't join us every day, for it's always cozy. Sometimes Marty's cross, which isn't a bit like her. It's just lately, though. And that Mrs. Tomlinson!" She shivered, "I don't understand her."

I don't really understand her myself, Charla wanted to say, but refrained. The woman had never unbent, and it created a cold atmosphere through which Charla hadn't been able to find her way.

For the most part, she noted, Mrs. Tomlinson seemed to help Mr. Craigie on special orders. Much of the time she was in a special room working with fabrics, and Charla noted that she was putting up orders of materials, checking the lists carefully, and giving directions to the shipping department on the handling of the great bolts of materials.

It occurred to Charlotte one day that the volume of business had increased a great deal since the first week or so. Maybe that was because spring and summer brought a demand for cotton goods.

She spoke of this at home, and her brother said, "Oh, yes, we always get a flurry of this in the spring months. Summer's deadly. Just you wait until late June and July and August. Of course the woolens start in during early fall, and the new patterns are pretty. By the way, Sis, pick yourself out some dress lengths of anything you want, and Jennie'll get her dressmaker to whip you up some new dresses."

She thanked him for his thoughtful generosity. "I don't need many things, Barrett, but thank you very much. I'll look around for something cool."

"Better do that tomorrow. We have a short season, and you'll want something for the Careys' garden party."

"That's right! I'd almost forgotten it."

"Better not, for she called this morning," said Jennie. "I'm going over for an hour or so. It's about two weeks from today."

As she rode into London the next morning, Charla recalled her brother's wish that she select some material and thought idly about colors. Something on a blue background with a white flower would be nice, or maybe pink. She'd have a look.

She thought of Jeff. He had called her one evening and had taken her for a ride and a dish of ice cream at the inn one

Sunday afternoon, but she hadn't seen him for several days. Occasionally on weekends, she saw him at a distance on his big horse. The Careys hadn't sent the promised horse over to Charla yet, because she had been too busy to ride him and asked that they delay it awhile. She really must get out for some more exercise.

It was eight-fifteen when she hung up her hat and jacket in the office. She decided, since it was a bit early and Mr. Craigie wouldn't get in for a while yet, she'd look for some material.

She went to the division of the showroom where the silks were on display. Bonnie was there dusting the counters and began to chat with Charla.

"Lookin' for something for yourself, dearie? I like that red print. Gives me quite a bit of a thrill. My gentleman likes red on me. But I durst not wear it to the shop, of course, so it's not a bit practical."

"Need we always be practical? Wake up and live dangerously!"

"Oh, Miss Gordon! Really you're quite funny, you know."

"Only at times! How do you like this blue silk with the large white flowers?"

"Not for me, but of course you could wear it," giggled Bonnie.

"It's a little heady even for me!" Charla searched the display. The lovely, frothy silks were gentian-colored, peach, tamarind, fuchsia, pearl-glo, wild honey, orchid, vibrant American beauty, the green of mist, the lilac of dusk! It was enough to confuse anyone.

Suddenly she spied the breathtaking loveliness of a blue different from any other shade on the tables.

Like a bee to a honey source, she flew directly to it. "It's Dior blue," she breathed. "Of course it is! I've seen it only once or twice at I. Magnin's. I mean this is really true, unmistakable Dior blue. Others copy it, but never quite get it." Charla stood there rapturously remembering the one dress that she'd wanted so badly, but had abstained from buying. That had been four years ago, when she was twenty and a little bit in love and he'd liked blue. She'd never bought another dress that color, although later she could have afforded one.

"Ducks, it's worth it, whatever it costs, to make you look like that. Me, I wouldn't want the white flower that's in it. Makes me look like an ale barrel. On you it'd be beautiful." Bonnie was wistful. "Here, Love, just take the whole bolt over and get Mrs. Madame to cut it for you. I'm never allowed to cut the expensive ones."

"I'll do it at noon, Bonnie. I want to think about it a little while. Mr. Craigie just came in, and I'll get it at lunch time." It was expensive, but it was like a cloud, and surely anything as delicate as a summer cumulous cloud in a blue sky — she could picture the Bay and the sky above San Francisco. The dress print had lovely white camellias splashed over it.

She hurried into the office, where Mr. Craigie was ready to give her a letter. It was to a large importer in the States. In fact, she recalled the address as being a street where a number of dress factories flourished in New York.

The letter was addressed to a Mr. Franklin G. Holmes, of A. S. Gold and Sons.

It was a routine letter, although she was surprised at the contents of the list which accompanied it. Gold and Sons seemed to be one of their very largest customers.

"This consignment of goods will reach you the week of the twenty-ninth and I suggest that you check it yourself," read the letter.

It ended with a request for a cablegram stating if Mr. Holmes found everything in order and that he would attend to the shipment himself.

A number of other letters were written during the day, and work went on. At lunch time Charlotte was delayed a bit longer than usual, although she had wanted to get back to the shop early. She walked about ten blocks for the exercise each day now and had lunch at a nearly hotel, the Mount Royal. Then she sometimes wandered in the vicinity of the Marble Arch, and sometimes shopped on the busy street near the Mount Royal.

Today she hurried through lunch, disregarding the questioning look of the head waiter who kept trying to press more selections upon her.

She found the other girls back at work and saw Mrs. Tomlinson at her accustomed desk, and decided to go over to the counter where she'd seen the lovely silk print, the Dior blue with the white camellias. She could picture the dress she'd have from the material.

She paused. The material was gone.

Oh, well, it had probably been put upon another table. She stood still, searching the other tables for it, but not another one carried it. Maybe it had been removed to a shelf.

She went up to Mrs. Tomlinson and said, "I found some silk on that table early this morning, and I'd like to buy some of it. It's a lovely blue with white camellias, a print."

"The blue and white print," Mrs. Tomlinson said rather grimly. "Oh, I see it." The tall angular woman took a few steps toward a table.

"No, not that blue print. I saw that, too, this morning, but this other silk is ever so much lovelier. I fell in love with it. It's a Dior blue, that gorgeous shade — "

"I think you're mistaken, miss. I see

no other blue, Dior or not, with white flowers on it. It's easy to get mixed up," she added more kindly, as though she saw the keen disappointment on Charlotte's face.

"But I'm not the least bit mixed up." A flash of resentment went over Charlotte. "I'm sorry. It must have been sold. Or has it been moved to another room?"

"Of course not! I'd remember. There just wasn't any other print, miss." Mrs. Tomlinson gave her head a quick, tempestuous nod and went back to her desk.

Charlotte walked angrily across the room. As she passed Bonnie, who was busy cutting and labeling, the girl whispered, "What's the matter with the old spavined cart horse?"

Charla broke into a light laugh, and the tension was broken. "It's nothing, Bonnie." She tossed the girl a bright smile. Why bother Bonnie?

She went on back to the office and worked industriously, putting the whole thing out of her mind.

She had formed a habit since the weather had turned warm of riding a bicycle into Kingston every morning, catching the bus and then, on her return from London, riding the bike back to Arden Manor. This left the little car for her sister-in-law, who really needed it to bring supplies home for the household.

Charlotte enjoyed the fresh air and the exercise, though her muscles were a bit sore the first few days.

Tonight it was a bit later than usual. She was riding along at a good clip, not paying much attention to the few cars which passed her. She rounded a curve and shot perilously near a car which suddenly turned right in front of her. She screamed, righted the bike, and shot past the car, which looked for all the world as though it were trying to run her down. The car roared past and a great moving van came down the highway. A familiar face had peered at her from the car.

The truck slowed as Charla stood on the pedals, white-faced and shaking, her bike poised on the brink of a vast drop below her.

"Help you, miss?"

She touched her brow, rubbing her hand across it. All she could think was that Mrs. Tomlinson had been in the car. But it had all happened so quickly.

The van driver got down and came over to her.

"Are you all right, miss? That was a narrow escape, wasn't it? Want me to haul you into the next town?"

"Thank you, no. I live just up the road a bit. I think I'll cut through the meadow."

She added wanly, "It was just an accident."

Her voice sounded unconvincing, and the man stared at her curiously. Well, she told herself as she thanked him and sat on her bike again, it really had been an accident, hadn't it?

7

MORE shaken than she'd realized, Charlotte developed a headache during the evening and left the other members of the family to retire early. She stood at her window for a while, looking out over the gardens, the fields in the distance and the small copse back of the gardens. The sun was down and the trees cast great shadows over the meadows.

She was thinking how much better the grounds looked than when she had first arrived. Mike, the gardener, was doing a fair job now, although she knew that he resented the supervision which her brother had asked her to give.

"He's not a really good gardener, but the only one we could get at the time. He works just part time usually, but now that everything's growing so fast he consented to stay." He had been working there for only three months when Charlotte came.

Charlotte, nervous from the near-accident on her way home, took a warm bath and curled up in bed to read a new magazine.

The words kept blurring together, and she could see Mrs. Tomlinson's face through the car window. The driver of the car had been a man. She had only a vague impression of him, but each time she saw him in memory, the lines around his tightened lips seemed deeper, his brows bushier and the intent more certain.

"I'm sure he tried to run me down," Charla said aloud.

What will you do about it? Will you ask Mrs. Tomlinson where she lives the next time you have a chance? Will you say casually tomorrow that you saw her last evening on the road? Or will you pretend that you haven't seen her?

To her surprise, Mrs. Tomlinson came into her office the next day and said in a friendly voice, "Miss Gordon, I went to the stockroom last evening to see if I could find the material you were interested in, but it must have been a mistake on your part."

"Why, thank you, Mrs. Tomlinson; that was most kind of you." Charla smiled. "It's easy to be confused about prints, when one sees so many at one time."

"I hope you'll find something else as pretty."

"Thank you. It was just an idea; I don't really need the dress."

Time passed quickly. Charla tried a new place to lunch, and about three o'clock she had a call from Iris Carey asking her to leave early and go to tea at Grosvenor House and then drive out home to Arden Manor with her.

It was a lovely day, and she couldn't be bothered with the gruesome thoughts of an accident!

Charla was glad she'd worn her best grey tweed suit and a pretty white blouse. She had a black bag and shoes and a smartly styled small grey hat with a tiny quill.

She took a cab to the hotel where Iris, accompanied by two other girls, was waiting for her. Since she'd had a good lunch, Charla felt she must turn down some of the pastry Iris had ordered.

But she felt warmed and pleased to be included with Iris' friends.

She was impressed by the service and by the hotel itself.

Charla listened with interest to the chatter of places and names now beginning to be familiar to her: Whitechapel Art Gallery, Royal Ascot, the Royal Order of the Garter at Windsor.

"One thing you must absolutely count on, Charla," said Iris, "is attending the annual regatta at Henley on the Thames."

"Yes, that's one of the musts. Oh, there are so many places to go and things to do!" Charla said. "I really haven't begun to do any of the things my brother and Jennie keep telling me about. Jennie has to stay with Barrett much of the time. But I'll be here six months at least."

"Tell us about Hollywood. Is it really like they say?" queried Rosemarie Heddon.

Charla smiled. Some of the things Europeans believed about America, and especially about Hollywood! Most people formed their ideas via the films shown at their local cinema. Talk swung suddenly to rumors about Vivien Leigh and her trip to New York.

"She was clever in Coward's *South Sea Bubble*, but best of all in her newest play."

After an hour of tea and small gossip, Iris said she had to get started. "Mums is having a special dinner tonight. It's their anniversary, and both Jeff and I promised to be on time."

They dropped the other two girls by their shared apartment and then, after stopping at her own place for her luggage, Iris drove out of the city a few minutes after six o'clock. It was a bad time to start, for traffic was heavy, but she was an expert at the wheel of her convertible.

"I tried to reach Jeff at his office, but he spent the day at Abingdale in court, so he's probably home by now." Iris turned her hazel eyes on Charla. "I think Jeff is quite impressed by you, Charla and Jeff is not easily impressed."

Charla blushed. Iris' direct gaze embarrassed her as much as the frank words.

"He has been very nice to me." Weak

words, but what would you say to a man's sister? After all, Jeff was fairly reserved, and probably wouldn't appreciate his sister discussing him.

Soon they were out on the less traveled road, and the time passed quickly. Charlotte felt a little ill as they passed the curve in the road near Arden where she had been so nearly involved in a crash the day before.

"I'll see you at Mum's garden party," Iris said, stopping the car in the drive.

"Yes, I'm coming over with Jennie."

"You'll be pressed into service, I think. Do you pour gracefully?" Iris grimaced. "I always manage to spill."

Two days later Jeff called and asked Charlotte to have dinner with him at the Savoy the next night and then to attend a play. "We'll dine early, if that's all right, so we can be on hand for curtain time. We'll sit in the stalls."

"Sounds like great fun, Jeff, and thank you," Charla said. She made a mental note to go into the office rather late in the morning, believing that she could still get there before Mr. Craigie.

However, she felt a little restless and slept uneasily. She rose at the usual time and dressed meticulously, wearing a sheath dress which would do for dinner, if she removed her jacket. It was a dark silk, sleeveless, with a beautiful neckline which took lovingly to pearls which she carried in her purse to be added just before leaving the office. The jacket had a crisply pleated small white collar and cuffs.

She felt excited and happy as her bus neared the corner of the London street where she always got off. Today would be one of the happier days she had spent in the unexciting atmosphere of Arden, Limited.

For once all she wanted was to have a gay evening.

The day passed without event. The same humdrum letters about materials, the orders to send through shipping, the chitchat of Marty and Bonnie as they prepared their tea which she shared during the morning.

She walked over to the tea room for lunch, which consisted of a small sandwich and two cups of strong coffee.

She paused and looked at the windows of a department store on the way back. She had done very little shopping since her arrival. Perhaps next week she would attend a fashion show at Harrod's, or go to Selfridge's and browse around at lunch time.

It was pleasant to have Bonnie come in about five o'clock and say, "There's a handsome young gentleman calling for you, Miss Gordon." Excitement brightened Bonnie's eyes and she was almost breathless for information.

"Oh, thank you, Bonnie. I'll be right along."

"I settled him in a nice big leather chair in the main showroom."

"Fine!" Charla took off her jacket and hung it on a padded hanger in her office cloak room. She clipped her pearls around her neck, added the lovely earrings.

"Gar! But you look beautiful, miss! Are those real pearls?"

"Just a reasonable facsimile. Do I really look all right?" Charla patted her hair, touched up her lipstick. "I didn't know he'd get here so soon."

"Is it nosy to ask if you're going out to dine?"

"It's the whole works — cocktails, dinner at the Savoy, a play at Her Majesty's Theatre, and home in the moonlight, with the top down on the convertible." She caught up her fur stole. "If it's warm enough, that is!"

"That'll be peachy. Have a good time, dearie, and I'll see you tomorrow at tea time."

She'd have to tell her all about it, too, Charla thought as she went out to meet Jeff.

He did look handsome, his blond, crisp hair shining in the desk light. He rose, tall and well groomed in a dark grey suit. No wonder Bonnie had been excited. It wasn't often, Charla told herself with humor, that the likes of a man such as Jeff graced these gloomy rooms.

They went down in the lift and out in the late afternoon to his car which he had managed to park nearby. They went first for cocktails at a favorite place he had spoken of, where they encountered a few people he knew. They spent perhaps an hour or so, and thence to the Savoy. It was still early, but a rising curtain at eight-thirty demanded concessions tonight.

"You're looking very pretty," Jeff said as they ate their soup. A mild compliment, but it caused her to feel a rush of warmth. "I've been planning on calling you to arrange for just such an evening for several days, but I get caught up in business and there you are! Actually, I have had the busiest spring I can remember since starting practice. Next week I'll be in Paris for two days."

"Sounds exciting!"

"Purely business. I'll fly, and hope to return in time for the party. By the way, Mother asked me to inquire if you'll assist between two and three?"

She nodded. "That sounds like fun, and I'll get to meet more people, probably."

They discussed the horse show, the tennis tournament and the possibilities of attending the Ascot races. She was thrilled to have Jeff ask her to go. It would be one of the most exciting events she'd ever attended, she told herself.

For at Ascot, one could see the Queen and Philip, perhaps glimpse Tony and Margaret.

As she barely tasted her dessert, Charla realized that the summer looming ahead of her suddenly seemed much more exciting than she'd thought possible.

8

THE play was not as hilarious as she had hoped a comedy would be, but entertaining enough so that they had several points to discuss on the way home. Charlotte had enjoyed the intermission, was intrigued with the serving of ices, drinks and pastries, so unlike American theatres.

She discoverd the stalls were very popular; although the dress circle wasn't nearly filled, seats were scarce in their own section. She wanted to learn more about the theatre in England. One could get a seat almost any time, there were so many offerings for the play-going public. It was a different matter at the cinema, she had discovered, noticing the long queue in front of the motion picture theatres.

The night was balmy and full of the fragrance of blooming trees and native shrubs which grew along the roadside. They slowed once and drove out on a lookout point to watch the reflection of the moon on the water. They didn't hear the thundering of the surf; otherwise Charla was reminded of the moon on the Pacific near Golden Gate Park.

Jeff lit a cigarette and smoked it before they went on, and they said but little.

It was rather late when they arrived at Arden. The night light in the drawing room was burning, and two lights were still on in the family wing upstairs. It was the first time that Charla had stayed on in the city for an evening out, and it had made a long day for her.

"Will you come in, Jeff?"

"It's too late, but maybe the next time. I'd like to have a chat with your brother soon."

"Why don't you come for tea on Sunday afternoon? Jennie'd love to see you, too."

"It's a date, then. About four?"

"Fine. And you might tell your father that I can take the horse he offered me any time now."

"I'll bring him over Saturday morning, it that's all right. We could try him out, if you'd like."

Thus in a few short days she saw considerably more of Jeff than she had expected. The ride through the hills near the vicinty of Arden was exhilarating. She didn't stay in the saddle too long, however, because she hadn't ridden for several years.

"He's a beautiful horse," she murmured, patting his silky dark coat. "Where did he get the name, *Vixen*?"

"From the fact that he was such a mischievous colt. He stole pastry out of cook's window one day. She named him unintentionally. It stuck, too. He was always annoying her, pulling her laundry from the line, and she had Father put an extra heavy lock on the paddock, for he always seemed to get out."

The children, Judith and Court, fell in love with Vixen and helped her take care of him. Now and then Mike would give him a rub-down and curry him, but Court liked to look after him, and often did so. The Gordons' stable consisted of only the two horses owned by Courtney and his father, and in the past Jennie had often ridden Courtney's.

The warm June days were passing rapidly, and the garden party at the Careys' was a high spot.

Molly, the Gordon's cook, baked some delightful tea cakes, decorated them with a surprisingly professional touch. Jennie and Charla, dressed in white, summery afternoon dresses, left for the party about one-thirty, hoping to help with some of the last minute details. Jennie had arranged a lovely basket of long-stemmed roses from her own garden. Charla carried a package of mints and one of salted nut confections as a little gift.

The children, Court and Judith, were going to come over about an hour later and have refreshments with several other children from the area. The Carey place was clipped, polished, and shining from the week-long preparations that had gone into the planning.

Several cars already stood in the parking area, and Charla noted Iris' convertible among them.

Jennie, parking beside it, said, "Iris did get home. She does seem a little frantic to me, rushing here and there;

I don't think her mother really knows where she is half the time. These modern girls!"

Charla laughed. "But it gives her a feeling of independence, Jennie. She has some rather nice friends, you know; such as the two girls I met. And I'm sure her parents approve the boy she goes around with. She'll settle down sometime and be just like her mother, the ideal English gentlewoman."

"Jennie, you look perfectly lovely, and you, too, Miss Gordon!" exclamied Mrs. Carey, opening the door for them. "And the roses, and the beautiful cakes! Molly called and said she was a wee bit disappointed!" She looked at them. "They couldn't be prettier, or taste better!"

"Agreed! Molly was just fishing for compliments! Now tell us what to do."

"Everything's ready. Thank you, dear," she said to Charla. "How thoughtful!" She read the label on the confections and looked her delight. "Will you please put them on the silver tray in the dining hall, and then come right on out to the garden?"

A few minutes later, Charla went out into the beautiful gardens and was excited by the beauty of the setting. Banks of flowers against old rock walls, new beds of roses, fountains splashing merrily in the sunlight, white stone benches, pretty tables arranged with colorful linen, a few gaily striped huge umbrellas, a croquet course, all might have been from the Victorian era.

People thronged in and out of the house and grounds for the next few hours. There seemed to be no let-up. Jennie was taken home by Iris, while Jeff came and helped Charla with the tea at her table.

A large-brimmed natural straw hat, with a swirl of tiny roses and fern and a flutter of black ribbon, almost hid her dark hair. She was wearing the white silk, over which were scattered a few large roses the color of the tiny ones on the hat.

As the last guest drifted away with her plate and there was a slight lull, Jeff whispered, "I say, you look beautiful in the garden frock and hat." He touched her white hand. "I've been trying to get around to telling you all afternoon, but with the dowagers hanging on every word, and all the gentlemen drifting back for more and more tea, I've had small chance."

"It's a lovely party," Charla said. "Your mother seems to have enjoyed every moment of it."

"Oh, she does! It's the biggest thing of the year for her. She likes the Christmas season, but here she really outdoes herself. It goes off so well that you'd never guess she plans out the smallest details as if it were military strategy." Jeff poised a delicate china cup on the fingers of his left hand. "Everything and everybody moves toward the day and the hour with the precision of the Changing of the Guard!"

Charla giggled.

"Iris just goes her merry way, but it used to be painful. How Mother ever got her here today I don't really know."

"But you seemed to enjoy it, Jeff. Were you bored?" she asked directly.

"Oh, not when I could keep my eye

on you. But I could have played polo today. Or I could have gone boating. Or," he bent down and spoke almost in a whisper, "we could have gone riding. I've found a new trail. Let's take our lunch next Saturday or Sunday, what do you say?"

"I'll have to check with you later in the week, Jeff."

"Can't you leave that tea tray now? I want to show you the summerhouse where Iris and I and the children of the servants used to pretend we were imprisoned."

She looked for a substitute to take her place, but there seemed to be no need, for most of the guests had now left, and there remained only an elderly couple who appeared to have settled down for the evening, talking with Mr. Carey over on a stone bench near a brilliant poppy bed.

Charla rose and took the arm Jeff offered. They strolled down a flagstone walk, and passed out of the main gardens to a series of smaller ones and thence through a stone-walled, sunken garden with grey steps and formal statues placed here and there among the rarer shrubs.

At the extreme end stood a round summerhouse of old, rosy brick, its walks sunken into deep velvety moss, the roof of the building, grey slate. Shutters at the open windows were painted a soft delphinium blue, matching the flowers in the closest bed.

"It's a quaint old place, romantic to some people, because it's been a favorite proposal site, a sort of idyllic rendezvous. Here, it has been said, my grandfather proposed to my grandmother; and here, it is also said, my father proposed to my mother. Iris used to bring her dolls up here and play by the hour."

Charla looked inside the building. Surprisingly, it was kept up as though in constant use. There were cane chairs, a reed sofa, a few tables, a small charcoal-buring stove equipped with a copper kettle, and a tea tray.

"I stayed up here during a storm one day, too scared to go to the house. It got dark, and I lit candles and was making myself a pot of tea when Father came. I never was so glad to see anyone!"

She could almost see a little boy,

frightenend but resourceful, struggling with the national drink which was a panacea for most ills in an Englishman's eyes.

They sat down on the bright chintz-covered sofa and chatted awhile.

Finally she rose, suggesting they start back to the house. "It's later than I thought," she said, looking at her watch. "My family's probably waiting for me at Arden."

"There's cold chicken and ham in the refrigerator. We could make sandwiches, if you're interested, or we could go to the Inn at Kingston."

She hesitated. Then she said, "Not tonight, Jeff, thank you. I promised Judith and Court I'd take them into the service tomorrow at the Abbey, so I must call it a day. And remember, you're coming for tea tomorrow afternoon."

"Yes, at four. I'll be there." They moved out of the house and into the old walk, strolling along as dozens of young people must have strolled through the centuries. Jeff directed her down a different path, and they paused on a small bridge spanning a rollicking little stream. A great green branch bent over the water, sheltering them.

Jeff turned to her, smiled, put his hands on her shoulders and drew her to him. He bent and kissed her lips.

9

CHARLA'S surprise must have been apparent to Jeff, she thought. But he turned her, his hand on her arm, and they walked on down the path as though nothing had happened. Her thoughts swirled. She had been kissed by boys before, but she had never made a habit of it.

He was speaking of the Ascot races, still to come up, and their plans to attend. On reaching the house, she made some parting comments to Jeff's parents but did not see his sister. Her car was missing from the parking strip when Charla and Jeff left. He drove rather quickly to Arden, and there was no reference to his kiss.

During the next two weeks she saw him frequently. They rode sometimes during the lovely evenings, sometimes on the trail through the woods on weekends. She attended the Ascot races with him, went to a tennis tournament where she met Iris and her friends once more. Occasionally she went with Jeff to see his parents or they drove over to Arden to visit with Barrett and his family.

At the shop in London, work moved on at a smooth, quiet pace. Nothing very exciting ever happened, she thought. The refined, dignified atmosphere, the reservation of Hugh Craigie and the kind but hardly friendly relationship between her and Mr. Maleky were not very conducive to cheer.

Bonnie took her vacation the first two weeks in July, and Marty followed the second half of the month. Mrs. Tomlinson seemed to be a permanent fixture. She was aghast when Charla asked her when she would have her time off.

"I've worked here five years now, and I've never so much as taken a day," she sniffed. "I'd like to know who'd look after my work if I was gone."

Charla was still working in Mr. Craigie's office, although at times when the girls were on their vacations she helped out in the sales, too. She therefore became acquainted with Harvey from the shipping department, and one day he asked her if she'd like to go through it. "It's a quiet day, miss, and some of the work's interesting, though mostly it's nailing up crates, putting them on the dollys and getting them out to the big trucks."

She was amazed to see the size of the operations. She had had no idea that the exporting end of the business was so large. Actually it didn't seem possible that the orders she typed for Mr. Craigie could add up to the shipments that seemed to be ready to go to the pier for ships to carry out of the harbor.

She knew, of course, that Mr. Maleky took charge of some of the exports, but she'd never realized that that office too, must be getting out many daily orders. Their customers were situated in many parts of the world.

This afternoon, though rather dull in the showrooms, was busy out here. Wide doors opening out to a big ramp disclosed two waiting trucks. Several men were busy at different chores, hammering box lids down, sorting, labeling, and marking the heavy cardboard signs with huge letters.

Harvey took her through a warehouse where she saw hundreds of shelves and their protected bolts of fabrics.

She spoke to her brother that evening about her surprise that the business was such a large operation.

He nodded. "It's been lots better for the past five years. Our overhead is huge, though, and shipping costs are almost prohibitive. We have lots of competition, too."

She wanted to ask when he'd had his books checked last, but that was really not her business. But that such a huge volume of business netted so small a profit was incomprehensible.

They'd enjoyed a particularly good dinner, cool summer breezes slightly blew the sheer curtains through their casements, and the children's cries and laughter from the tennis court drifted into the room. Jennie, knitting a white wool sweater, looked pleasantly matronly under the bright light near her chair.

Barrett was able to move around the room a little with the aid of crutches; in about a month, he was to be fitted with an artificial leg.

Usually during an evening such as this, no reference at all was made to Barrett's disability. She had learned how to avoid and head off the approach of such conversation.

"We can never thank you enough for coming to our assistance, Charla," Jennie said. "The whole household has benefited from your presence," Jennie went on. "Kit is doing better work; Molly hasn't fussed at her for several weeks. Even Mike seems to keep the stables cleaner and do the yard work more willingly. The vegetables are looking great. He seems to take pride in them. Vixen shows good care. Last evening when I went for a ride with Judith and Court, their horses appeared to be in good condition, too. Of course, I know that Court does a good job with them, as he should."

"A boy of eleven!" Barrett sighed. "Sometimes I think I expect too much of him. He's still in Lower Form, you know. Tell me, Little Sis, was I as backward in math as Court seems to be?"

She laughed. "Truthfully, you were no

shark, if that's what you wanted to hear. But you did give me a helping hand in Algebra, I recall. I think Court will snap out of it."

"I sincerely hope so," said her brother. "I hope he'll want to go right into the Arden company. But maybe by that time he'll not need to understand math. All these robots may make his work into child's play."

"I don't think one can sell a reluctant customer a bolt of fabric, though," said Charla.

"They're getting cannier every day," laughed Jennie. "How about some music?" She moved over to the hi-fi and began looking for favorite records.

The two children came in from tennis presently, still arguing about the outcome of their last set.

"Okay, okay, so I'll challenge you to a game the first thing in the morning!" said Court, wiping beads of perspiration.

"Done!" cried his sister.

"Time for you two to go up and get your showers. Then you can come back down for a few mintues," said their mother.

"Please! Please let us have ten minutes with Charla."

"Very well, but don't get close. No, don't try to hug her, Court! Both of you go on and shower, then come back!"

Tanned and long-legged in their tennis shorts, they were the picture of glowing health. Without delay they left the room, still arguing on the stairs.

Charla, listening to the music, feeling the soft breeze drifting through the window, aware of the fragrance of the roses which filled the room, closed her eyes.

A few minutes later the two children appeared and asked for a cake and some milk. Jennie started to rise, but Charla said quickly, "Let me help them. I know where everything is and just how Molly wants things put away."

The three of them walked down the long hall to the kitchen and Charla turned on the light. Everything was in excellent order, as it always was. The floor gleamed with a high coat of polish. Kit usually mopped the blue and white linoleum and took care of the halls, too. Molly considered the kitchen as her domain, excepting when it came to the scrubbing of the floors and the window washing.

They peeped into the pantry. "I'm sure Molly put a tray of small cakes in here, probably for tomorrow's tea. But you may each have one." Charla opened the cupboard and withdrew the covered tray. "Here you are, and now for the milk."

"You know, we think you're a brick, Charla," said Court. "It was very nice of you to come and help us out. Do we make much trouble for you?"

"Of course not! What ever gave you such an idea?"

"Kit said we mustn't. She said American girls are rich and never have to do things like this unless they want to."

Charla smiled. "Not very many American girls are rich. And most of us work pretty hard."

"The cinema shows girls who have beautiful gowns and ride in big, long cars and live in beautiful apartments."

"Those are just story book characters. Some English girls have all that, and better than that. I've never really had a home where we had a maid, a cook and a gardener, especially one who would take me to school and come get me!" smiled Charla.

"Oh, you mean Mike? How else would we get there?"

Charla shook her head. "I just don't know. Now, drink up and let's get on back for that last ten minutes!"

"You know, Charla, speaking of Mike," said Judith slowly, "I heard him talking about you to Kit the other evening. He wanted to know as much about you as she could find out. I wanted to tell Mother, but I thought it might worry her. He said to find out how long you were going to stay, and who you knew in London, and if you got any letters from America to find out who they were from."

"Judith!"

"I know. I really didn't mean to listen, but I was sitting in the summerhouse, and Kit had brought Mike some lemonade while he was working in the flower garden."

"He might have seen you! It's such a fragile little house, all trellises and screen."

"Now, whatever would he want to

know all that for?" queried Court.

Judith shrugged her shoulder. "I don't know."

"Let's just keep it a secret and don't say anything to anyone. Thank you for telling me, Judy." Charla set away the pitcher and washed their glasses.

"Just one more thing, Charla. Mike said something about an accident on the road. I thought he said something about your bike, but I knew that was impossible."

Charla suddenly halted. How could Mike have known about that near-accident that evening several weeks ago? She shrugged. He might have been working in a field nearby. But she couldn't dismiss the conversation from her mind, and it disturbed her all evening. She would be careful with her letters. She didn't relish the thought of Kit going through her things.

10

THE next evening, on going up to her room immediately following dinner, Charlotte found Kit turning away from her dressing table as she entered.

"Oh, miss! I didn't hear you. I was just tidying up a bit for you. A little powder was spilled here and there."

Charlotte looked at her searchingly. "I thought you were to come in to sweep and dust in the mornings, Kit." She was able to speak in a quiet tone, although her heart had suddenly begun to pound. It was perfectly obvious that the maid had been going through the drawer that stood slightly open.

"Sometimes when you come in a bit late, and I think maybe you've had to change in a hurry, I check on your room, and I always turn your bed down."

Of course she did. But that wasn't usually done until about nine.

"Isn't it a bit early for that?"

"No offense, Mum. I'm going out with my gentleman this evening. We thought we'd just ride into Abingdale to the cinema. Hardly ever get to go that far." A little whining plea was in her last words. She didn't look Charla right into the eye.

An idea came to Charla. She simply must not let Kit realize that she suspected her of anything. "It's all right, Kit. I can turn my bed down tonight, and I don't ever mind doing it, so you won't need to come in from now on."

"Oh, but Mrs. Gordon wouldn't like that. She's very watchful to see I do my work, miss. Cook would be sure to know, too." She finished turning down the light quilted cover. "Good night, miss. Is there anything I can do for you tomorrow? I'll be helping with the laundry."

"Thank you. I'll put out my lingerie, as usual." Charla hesitated and added, "Have a pleasant evening, Kit."

The sallow face lit up. "Why, thank ye, Mum. It's a good picture, one of my favorite stars."

After the girl had gone, Charla drew a long breath. She opened the drawer.

There were only a few white linen handkerchiefs, a hosiery box, a small plastic container for curlers. "Small pickings! She'd have difficulty making anything out of that. I know Jennie wouldn't keep her if she thought Kit was going through the dressers."

The next evening she brought a gift to Kit and one for Molly. She had found a lovely white silk slip for Kit, and she purchased a lavender woolen scarf, a sort of cape stole, for Molly.

She handed each of them her package following dinner when they were just ready to leave the kitchen. "I want you to know I appreciate everything you've done for me since I came," Charla said warmly. She had given them tips, but somehow a personal gift seemed more suitable.

Cook was very pleased. A dark pink flush stained her heavy cheeks. "Now, isn't that just like you, Miss Charlotte? I'll wear it to meetings. Thank you, dearie, thank you."

Kit took a long time unwrapping her package. "You needn't have, miss. You needn't have at all." She lifted the white shimmering silk from its tissue. "It's the prettiest one I ever had, miss, and I'll keep it for my wedding day, if I ever have one."

Charla smiled and said lightly, "No, don't keep it. Wear it, and if I'm around I'll buy you another slip for your wedding. Will it fit?"

"Just right, and I do thank you, miss." Kit held it up to her chambray dress, careful not to let it touch. "It's exqueesite, miss, perfectly exqueesite."

Charla escaped from them and went on about her business. She had letters to write, including one to Greg, whom she'd been neglecting again. It was difficult to find time, there were always so many things of interest to do. Jeff was in Paris again, this time for four days, and so she found her evenings bereft of their usual excursions either by horseback or in the car.

The next day at the office she turned through a fashion magazine with coordinating styles and patterns which had reached her desk. She suddenly decided to look again among the fabrics and see if she could find the Dior blue with the white camellias she was certain she'd once seen. The search netted her no result, except the realization that the silk print was not among the most recent materials on display. She had kept her eyes open week after week, but unless she went right into the showroom and purposely hunted, she knew that it might not catch her eye. Bonnie had watched for it, also, having backed her up with the assertion that she, too, had seen the white camellia print, the one on the beautiful blue background.

Neither had made a point of discussing it with Marty because she had been on her vacation when the incident happened. It was a sort of secret between them, and Bonnie would have been most happy to prove Mrs. Tomlinson wrong.

Three days later she was surprised to see the material in an unopened bolt on a shelf in the storeroom. She had been sent to take a list to Harvey and, finding him busy at the moment, stood waiting for him, her eyes traveling over the huge bolts of fabrics.

"That's it! That's just exactly what I want," she said aloud.

"What's that, Miss Gordon?" asked Harvey. "Sorry to keep you waiting."

"It doesn't matter. Here's a list of orders, Harvey. Mr. Craigie wants you to get them out by this evening if possible." She handed him the list and took a step away. She almost asked him to get the bolt of goods down for her and to take it to the showroom, but decided against delaying any of the employees on a personal chore.

"I saw the white camellia pattern again, Bonnie," she said in a low voice. "It's in the storeroom. I'll have a dress from it. It's a little late in the season, but it's so pretty, and I can wear it through the winter if I have a jacket made of the same material."

"Indeed you can, miss. We'll see about it at noon."

"Okay, we'll do that."

She'd said absolutely nothing to Mrs. Tomlinson about it.

She was trying to figure out just how she could manage to have a dress length cut from it, when Mrs. Tomlinson was the person who usually cut the expensive silks. Charlotte pushed the problem out

109

of her mind and went on taking dictation from Mr. Craigie. It was one of the busiest days they'd had in a long time, and so she was rather late going out for lunch. When she returned, Bonnie was already back at work, and Charla decided she'd take a later bus that evening and bear her material triumphantly home with her.

At last when the final page was typed and the envelope sealed, she closed her typewriter with relief. Mr. Craigie had already left the shop. Charlote stood up and stretched a bit. Her shoulders felt cramped and she was a little depressed. It had been a warm day. On such a day as this, back in her San Francisco office, the weather conditioner would have been turned on.

She crossed the display room on the way to the lavatory to wash and get ready to catch the late bus. She paused as she remembered her plans somehow to get the material and take it home with her. She glanced over at Mrs. Tomlinson's desk, and saw the older woman, her dour face almost hidden by the brim of the large-brimmed black straw hat she'd just donned. She drew on her black nylon gloves, buttoned her jacket and turned the key in her desk. She was leaving.

Charla went on into the lavatory. Bonnie was touching up her lips with a bright pink lipstick.

"Late tonight, huh? Thought I'd never get through. Old Mrs. Clabber kept bringing me more and more work after the usual closing hour."

"I just remembered that material. How'll I ever get it cut off the piece?"

"Gar! I don't know. She'll kill me if I cut it. I never have, you know. Marty might. She does once in a while, but not me!"

You really are a frightened rabbit! thought Charlotte. But of course, since I can't do it myself, I can't really blame you. Yet Barrett had said she could make any selection she wished.

She'd go get the fabric, tell Barrett about it, simply lay it on the desk in her office tonight, and have Mrs. Tomlinson cut it for her in the morning. That was the sensible, the proper way to do business. After all, her brother and sister-in-law owned Arden, Limited, didn't they?

"Go with me, Bonnie, to the storeroom?"

"Well, sure. I'm a little late, but what's it get me anyhow when I get home early? Just a passel of bawlin' brats and Ma not doin' nothin' about it."

Charla shuddered inwardly. No wonder Bonnie wasn't allowed to cut the delicate materials.

They turned on the lights in the storeroom. By now everyone seemed to have left. The clang of the steel doors on the big ram down in the shipping room sounded with a note of finality, announcing the day was over.

Up one aisle and down another. "It's over here, Bonnie. Should be in this next aisle. Here we are. It was right across from Harvey's old desk."

She snapped on the nearest light, which sent out a bright gleam into the dusk of the corner. "Let's see now; it's just one or two rows over — " she broke off. Staring unbelievingly she murmured, "It can't be. It just can't be gone!"

But it was.

"It's probably in the display room," said Bonnie.

"Of course, but only over Mrs. Tomlinson's dead body."

But it wasn't there, even if it did seem logical for it to have been moved into the room where customers looked over the materials. The two girls searched table after table; they went into the smaller rooms, through the shelves, over the counters. As though it had never existed, the fabric was missing.

"Well, I'll be darned! I'll just plain be darned."

"You probably wanted it so badly that you just thought you saw it," said Bonnie soothingly.

"Of course!" Charla answered brightly.

She and Bonnie went back into the cloak rooms, and presently left the quiet floor and went down to a busy London street.

"Good night, Bonnie. Please keep mum. Anyone would think I'm balmy, wouldn't they?"

"Don't 'ee worry that pretty little head, dearie." said Bonnie. "Get a good night's sleep, and I'll take tea with you tomorrow."

"Right." And of course a cup of good hot tea would fix everything.

The next day as she was coming into Mr. Craigie's office she heard a reference to the white camellia pattern. "Of course I can send it. It's on standing order from the mill. The Dior blue with the camellia."

Mr. Craigie whirled his chair around as she made a slight noise. She thought he looked guilty. "I'll be in touch," said Craigie into the telephone.

"Do you want something, Miss Gordon?" The clipped voice sounded disapproving, but then it frequently did. He studied her face, and she hoped she gave no sign that she'd heard. "I didn't ring for you." She knew instantly that he was angry.

"I'm sorry, sir. I wanted to check this order. Is there another listing somewhere in your files? This seems incomplete."

She was consumed with curiosity about the white camellia pattern. Suddenly she saw no reason she couldn't ask about it.

They finished the item she had come in to inquire about, and she said, "Mr. Craigie, my brother has given me permission to select some dress lengths. I'd like to have one from the fabric you were discussing when I came in. I saw it when I first came and asked about it, but Mrs. Tomlinson was sure I'd made a mistake about the print, for we couldn't find the silk later. The whole bolt seemed to have disappeared. I saw another or perhaps the same one, when I went to the shipping room for you yesterday afternoon. May I have about four yards of it?"

"I'm not at all sure which material you're referring to."

"The Dior blue with the white camellia print. You just now referred to it."

"Miss Gordon! Are you in the habit of listening to your superiors?" His thin words issued from thin lips. "I prefer you to discuss this with the employees who handle such matters," he added from a lofty pinnacle.

"Yes, thank you," she said quietly. She moved quickly to the door. Two crimson spots burned high on her cheeks. She was not through with the subject by any means.

11

BY now Charla was thoroughly disturbed about the white camellia print on the blue background. She could not erase it from her thoughts. She actually no longer cared whether or not she had a dress length from it by the end of the week, for it continued to haunt her.

Bonnie mentioned it at tea on Friday during the morning recess and Marty was all ears. She had not been aware of the fact that a little mystery was being enacted right in their shop and appeared to be interested as the average shopgirl might be.

Two things happened over the weekend to frighten Charla, but she did not relate them to the white camellia print until several weeks later.

As she rounded the drive on her bicycle, coming back from the village where she'd ridden for some last minute things for Sunday dinner, she encountered

Mike quite suddenly. It gave her a peculiarly eerie feeling that he'd been waiting for her; it was almost like an ambush. She smashed into the light cart he was pushing. He had suddenly appeared crossing the drive, with gardening tools piled in the cart, to do some work on the flower beds near the house.

The violent impact sent Charla catapulting from her bicycle, but she luckily went out to the side, landing on the grass instead of the driveway itself. She narrowly missed the sharp prongs of the steel fork and, for that matter, the rake.

The breath knocked completely out of her, she lay there, and an icy feeling washed over her as she saw the sharp points of steel she had so narrowly missed.

"Miss, are you hurt?" Mike bent over her solicitously.

The dark lashes fluttered down over Charla's white cheek. The pain in her diaphragm was agonizing, and for another moment she was unable to rise.

There was a sudden scream from her niece. Judy came flying down the drive, and presently Court and then Jennie were there.

Mike knelt beside her and slipped his arm under her neck, but Jennie said, "Wait; don't move her yet."

A tiny bit of color was coming back into Charla's cheeks, and she managed to pull herself up a bit; then the gardener helped her to a sitting position.

"I'm that sorry, miss! Truly, I should have been watching closer."

"You could have killed her!" said Jennie sharply. "Oh, dear Charla, I do hope there are no broken bones."

Charla managed a wan smile. She shook her head. Breathing was a bit easier now. "I think I'm all right," she panted.

Looking at the long prongs of the pitchfork, she shuddered.

"Isn't that a dangerous way to carry those tools?" Jennie asked quietly. "With two children and others in the household, you must observe all precautions for safety."

Mike touched his hat brim. "Yes, Miz Gordon. I was in a hurry and just didn't think. I'll be more careful in the future."

Jennie nodded. "Court, pick up the packages, please. Now don't try to walk yet, Charla." She glanced at the bicycle with its handlebar twisted. "Well, that's out of commission, and maybe a good thing, too."

Charla thought ruefully, I'll have to take the car to the bus station next Monday.

Presently she was able to walk up to the house and found that, except for the loss of her breath and a few minor scratches, she had been very, very lucky. She daubed the cuts with a germicide and went on up to her room to wash and make herself presentable. Wearing bright blue slacks and a striped tee shirt after a quick shower, she went downstairs again so as to reassure to Jennie that she was really unhurt.

Jennie was preparing a gelatin salad for dinner, with Molly casting a look at it now and then. The older woman was basting the beef roast, and the kitchen was filled with the aroma of good foods.

"That Mike!" clucked Molly. "I'm not so sure about him, Mum, if you'll pardon me saying so. Careless, that's what he is. I never have liked his looks, and don't mind telling you that he isn't much help to Kit."

"Hasn't she been doing her work well?" Jennie asked.

"Slipped back a little, if you ask me. I hope you're none the worse for wear, Miss Gordon."

"Thanks; only a few scratches and a bruise or two. I'm lucky to be so bouncy." Jennie sat down weakly at the table.

"I've some hot tea, dearie. It'll make you feel better. Shall I just pour you some, even if it isn't time?" asked Molly.

Jennie came over by Charla's chair. "Are you sure you're all right, Charla? You're still quite pale."

"Yes. I was just remembering those horrible prongs on that fork and how narrowly I missed hitting it."

Molly nodded. "Gives one a real bad turn. Here, now, drink this. It'll do you good."

It did her remarkably much good, she thought, smiling a little after sipping the strong, hot brew.

Dinner was served out on the patio later in the evening. By mutual agreement no one mentioned Charla's fall to her brother, although it came out later that night when Court referred to it. But by that time Charla was her old normal self and none of her bruises showed. Her scratches were mainly on her upper arm, easily covered by her jacket.

The next morning Charla went into the nearby town, Abingdale, driving the children to church, as Jennie had elected to stay home with Barrett. It was one of those breathtakingly lovely Sunday mornings; the remaining dew sparkled on the grass, birds twittered in the huge branches of the old trees, and the blue of the Thames was entrancing.

On the way home from the services, Charla pulled off the main road and they sat and watched some of the small boats on the river. Picknickers with hampers and eternal sun umbrellas strolled in a green park nearby. Tables were already covered with bright cloths.

The two children and Charla discussed the advantages of a small boat, and she knew they longed to have one. But it would be useless to discuss it with her brother.

They arrived back at Arden Manor about one-thirty. The Sunday mid-day meal was to be served at two.

"How about going out for a ride this afternoon, Auntie?" Court asked.

"That'll be just fine, if I can manage to sit in the saddle. I'll confess that my muscles are a bit sore today."

"We can go next week," said Judith.

"It's been quite a while since we've gone together, just the three of us," said Charla. "I tell you what. I have a few letters, and Jeff is coming over for late tea and a game of chess with your father. I think we can get in a little run about four. Will you saddle Vixen for me, Court?"

"Sure thing! I'll curry him for you, too."

"Good boy. It'll be fun. I always enjoy riding with you two. It's a nice summer, isn't it, kids?"

Court flashed a smile at her. "It would have been rather boring without you, though. Father usually takes us on a bike trip one week, you know."

"Yes. They'll be nice to remember."

Memories were good to cling to, especially the pleasant ones. She grimaced a bit as she got out of the car. She hoped she'd ride well this afternoon. If Jeff rode over on his horse instead of driving his car, they might encounter him!

Barrett was in a very pleasant mood at the dinner table. The setting was quite festive, the linens were new, and Charla noticed that Jennie had embroided an elegant old English G in a corner of each napkin. The simple but beautiful touch gave the children a sense of belonging; some day, if they took good care of this set, perhaps Judith's children would be using the napkins and cloth. It gave one a feeling of continuity. The crystal sparkled and the heavy silver was highly polished and quite practical.

Mike was cutting firewood for the fireplaces today. They could hear the whirr of the saw through the open window. Of his own volition, too. They didn't expect him to work on Sunday afternoon, at least not at any major project. It flashed through Charla's mind that Mike was on his best behavior, probably truly regretting yesterday's incident with the garden cart.

"I'll help Mike stack the wood as soon as I 'tend Vixen," volunteered Court.

"That's fine, Court. I appreciate all of the help you've been around the place this summer," said his father.

A slight blush stained the boy's cheeks. "I'm glad to help Mike. He'll help me saddle the horses, maybe."

"Can't you manage them alone? I wouldn't interrupt his work, son."

"Oh, sure, I do it all the time. I like to work with the horses."

The table talk drifted to coming social events of the next few weeks, and the children's week at a summer camp in early August.

"One thing I've not mentioned to you, Charla," said her brother as dessert was served. "There's a fashion show in Paris in the offing for you, if you'd like to go."

"Would I? Oh, Barrett! How wonderful!" she gasped.

"It will be very exciting," said Jennie. "I went with Barrett one year. We furnish some of the designers with materials.

You'll have a marvelous time, Charla. I can't think why we haven't discussed it before, It's in mid-August. There's another in November which you'll love, too; there's no reason for you not to represent the company, is there, Barrett?"

"Of course not! I've planned all along for her to go. It's just that I get so busy with current things."

Judith was excited and asked if sometime she'd be able to go, maybe next year when she looked more grown up.

"There's a lot of time for that, Pet," said her father.

The plan opened a whole new vista for Charla, she thought as she went upstairs to put on her jodhpurs. She eased herself into them a bit tenderly, but decided that she'd be able to ride. She stood tall and slim in the riding habit: a white silk shirt, open at her tanned throat, a dark green fitted jacket, matching cap and the jodhpurs.

On the way downstairs, she heard the hall clock striking four, and so she went directly out the door to go to the stables. The tall trees cast leafy shadows across the velvety grass. Mike was still cutting wood down close to the stables, and she could hear the engine of the little saw as it whirred in the stillness of the Sunday afternoon. Judith had gone down ahead of her, and she could hear the children's voices as she walked down the narrow flagstone walk.

Judith was already in the saddle of her smaller horse, and Court was waiting to give his aunt a lift.

"Oh, Vixen looks wonderful! Thanks, Court, for currying him." She withdrew a cube of suger from her pocket and, going up, gave it to the horse. She patted the lovely sensitive head, reached for the bridle, gave her foot to her nephew. She eased herself into the saddle gently, feeling the soreness caused by yesterday's fall from the bicycle.

Court mounted and the three were off. As they passed Mike, the boy called to him, and the gardener waved a hand but continued to work. He didn't even glance at Charla. He's embarrassed about yesterday, of course, she thought.

They walked the horses to the edge of the meadow and Court opened the big white gate. They chose a narrow country road, off the main traveled highway and trotted the horses at a fairly good clip.

"Feel like racing, Auntie Charla?" called Court.

"Of course not; don't you remember yesterday?" said Judith indignantly.

"I think I can take it," said Charla.

"I'm sorry. We can race next time."

"I challenge you!" cried Charla, knowing his disappointment. "From here back to the meadow gate, and no holds barred!"

"Righto!" shouted Court. "Shall we jump the hedge?"

"Certainly. I'm no sissy. Beat you at your own game."

"I don't think you ought to jump today," said Judith gravely.

"I'm really quite all right, Judy dear. Don't worry about me. Pooh! Anyone can take that little hedge."

The moment she took the hedge, Charla regretted it. She felt a sudden slip, and plunged over Vixen's head out of the saddle. Stunned, she lay quietly.

She could hear Court's stricken voice. "Oh, Charla, Charla, it was the saddle! But I fixed it just like always."

"I'm all right, Court. Hush, Judith. I'm all right, I tell you."

The girl's sobs were almost hysterical. She bent over her aunt, touching her white forehead.

"How beastly! How beastly! I'll never forgive myself," said Court. Tears were running down his tanned cheeks, and Charla knew she had to sit up, no matter how gingerly.

"Two times in two days!" sobbed Judith. "Are you sure you're not broken in two?"

Charla shook her head. "No, I'm really not hurt at all. Must have been that tumbling course I took in P.E., my dears."

"No, wait now. I'll get back of you and let you brace youself against me. Slow and easy, Auntie."

She felt the security of his strong young arms around her waist. She gasped. "You know, I really am all right. How can anyone be so lucky twice?"

Vixen, as though suffering great remorse, had come back to them and was standing near the low hedge, his saddle dragging on the ground.

"Can you walk, Charla?" asked Judith anxiously.

Her Aunt took a tentative step. "I think so."

"Bring my horse, Court, and help her up on him, and I'll lead her back to the house. Can you get into the saddle, Charla?"

Charla looked a little sick. "I think I'd rather walk."

"No, don't be afraid. The best thing to do is to ride. Get right back up on the horse and go along as though nothing had happened. It's the only thing to do," admonished Judith.

12

COURT was so quiet going back to the stables, that Charla with quick compassion said thoughtfully, "Now let's please not mention the fall to your parents. It would only worry them, and no harm is done."

"Court ought to be ashamed of himself," said Judith.

"Don't dear. He feels awful. Please don't make it worse. It'll never happen again," Charla said in a low voice.

Court was so subdued the remainder of the evening that she was pleased when he decided to go to his room early and do some work with his junior chemistry set. Judith had been watching television from the study, and Jennie and Charlotte watched the men's chess game. Charla had changed from her riding clothes into a blue chiffon frock and, although still a bit pale, hoped she appeared normal to the others.

Jeff stayed rather later than usual that

evening, and the last hour they spent listening to some new records shipped to her by a San Francisco shop with whom she had left a special order.

Charla told Jeff about the plan for her to go to Paris the following month.

"That's great!" he exclaimed. "I may manage to make a necessary trip, and I'd get to take you around in that fabulous city."

He told her of some of the places she should visit.

She said breathlessly, "But I'll have to spend much of my time in the showrooms. Maybe I could stay over the weekend, however."

"You must, especially if I can arrange to be there, too."

Later as she got ready for bed, she thought, "I've never been to Paris, and now to get to go and to be escorted by Jeff! It's almost too exciting to be true.

Caught up in the busy day at the shop on Monday, she almost forgot her sore bruises. She didn't mention the incidents to either of the two girls, avoiding the time for tea in the morning and knowing that they really never expected her in the afternoon. She simply didn't care for tea that late in the day. If she had it, she didn't feel hungry enough for dinner.

Mr. Craigie had returned to his old, quiet, highly dignified manner, and she had almost forgotten the episode of his accusing her of eavesdropping on a telephone conversation. He seemed even friendlier than usual the next two weeks, and when she told him that her brother was sending her to Paris to attend the openings he was quite nice about getting a substitute for her, arranging it through a local employment agency.

Relieved, she began to plan her wardrobe for her trip, and was pleased to find that she really needed to shop for one or possibly two garments. She bought a transitional dress from the gown room at Harrod's, paying for it with money that her brother had insisted was part of the expense fund for the trip.

Iris drove her brother and Charlotte to the London airport prior to their departure to Paris. She was in a rare gay mood and had insisted on taking them in. They had decided to leave on a Sunday morning so they could be ready for the festivities preceding the opening of the Dior show.

Charla had tickets for several interesting events, and as a special hospitality, she had received two for each.

Jeff was going to be a wonderful companion for evenings and the weekend, she thought gratefully as he solicitously fastened the seat belt before their take-off. It was a clear, beautiful day, and she enjoyed every moment of the flight. They landed at Orly and took a cab to her hotel, off the Rue De La Paix, symbol of Parisian elegance.

Charla craned her neck at all the lovely color of Paris, so different from the grey of London. Here the wide streets, the cheer of the passing throngs, the very color of the stone and brick buildings fascinated her. The cab driver passed the landmarks, the Opera House, the Arc de Triomphe, slowly, so that she got her first look at them. There would be so much to see, so much to do. She thought of herself as disembodied, as merely a shell, going through the ordinary routine of travel, but with her mind darting here and there, in perpetual motion. She had to see the interiors of all those famous places: the Louvre, the Invalides, Eiffel Tower, the Tuileries Gardens, Sainte Chapelle, the Bastille, Luxembourg Palace — she could name a dozen more that she must visit before the week ended.

Just as they drew up in front of her hotel, Jeff murmured, "We have a date to dine at Maxim's tonight, remember. I'll make the reservation for eight, if that suits you?"

"Fine."

"How about a ride on the Seine this afternoon? We can lunch, and then go out about three, and that way you can get a wonderful picture of the buildings which overlook the river."

"Sounds perfectly wonderful. Oh, Jeff, would I seem immature if I do a lot of sight-seeing?"

"Certainly not. That's why I made special arrangements. I want to show you Paris, Charlotte. It has a very special meaning, I understand, if shown to a person in the excitement of a first look."

She was grateful for his help through customs, and his thoughtfulness as he looked after her. He kept the cab waiting for himself as he saw that she was checked in properly.

"I'll stay at the Astor, for I have a due bill there. I handle some of their London business for them. It's only a few blocks away from here," he had told her.

Her hotel was very old, but very fine, and she appreciated the impeccable service. It was the extra, the thoughtful little touches that she would always remember. Her room was quite large. The wall bed was let down every night by the maid, made up and ready for her to retire when she returned from her evening engagements. All day the room was an elegant drawing room, with a handsome leather-topped desk, provincial in design, a deep piled carpet of luxurious quality, as were the large colorful towels and the coverings of the furniture. Her 'wardrobe,' an elaborately carved piece of furniture, amazed her by its capacity. Rather quaint, she thought, summing it all up, but a wonderful experience.

Jeff called for her about two o'clock and they walked down to a small sidewalk café for lunch in the bright sunshine.

She had lunched once at Greenwich Village at a sidewalk table, and now she enjoyed watching the strollers and the flow and ebb of Paris on a bright sunny afternoon.

They took a boat ride on the Seine later. They sat on the top deck and watched the rushing of the waters over the side, enjoyed the shade of the trees, throwing their shadows into the river.

On the way back to her hotel, they strolled slowly past some of the beautiful shops on the Rue De La Paix. She recognized many of the world's most famous designers' names. The accessories displayed with the models were breathtaking.

She knew she would be enjoying much of the same sort of thing on the following day, and fearing it might be boring Jeff, she moved on a bit faster.

"You really don't need to rush. I enjoy all of this, too," he said understandingly. "With Iris and my mother both interested in clothes, I've had a bit of training in window shopping."

"I'm just like most females, interested in clothes. I enjoy seeing the unusual more than I'd enjoy wearing it. I'll confess that raising and lowering hemlines is not one of my chief hobbies."

She thought he looked pleased. Most Englishmen, she had long ago decided, hoped their women would look 'ripping, old boy,' but in a sort of dignified English manner. This must surely account for the somber clothing colors, the tweeds, the sturdy shoes, the practical side of the English modes.

Dinner at Maxim's was another experience she would long remember, she thought as she got ready for bed a little before midnight. Her first day in Paris! And there were to be at least five more of them, the weekend if she decided to stay.

Jeff would be going back to London on Thursday; he had been unable to stay longer. "Although I just might be persuaded to come back," he'd added when he'd told her that morning.

"I'll probably be so dead on my feet by Friday night that I'll just wait until Saturday to get a plane back to London," she told him. There were to be two showings each day, and they would consume the mornings, luncheon periods and the afternoons until four. Most of the early evenings there would be invitations for cocktails, and one night there would be a composite.

She had two appointments scheduled with designers from Mlle. Mousore. She was only thirty, but her establishment already had an unusual reputation, and Barrett had been anxious to sell to that house.

Some sample cases had arrived before she had, and they now stood within touch of her bedside table. She started to look again at some of the exquisite fabrics, then firmly closed the lids and settled back on her pillow.

Her bedside telephone rang and she answered rather sleepily.

"Hello, Charla. I just wanted to see how you've fared your very first day in Paris," said Jeff's voice.

"Just wonderful, Jeff. And again, I do thank you for taking such good care of me. It was lots of fun."

"We'll continue it tomorrow evening, then? I can get away early, if you want to attend that cocktail party."

"I'll attend one later, but not the very first opening day. I'd lots rather have a cup of tea with you on the Rue De La Paix"

"Very well. I'll pick you up at the showroom at the Hilton about four. Or is that soon enough?"

"Just right. I can wire Barrett or call him if there's anything pressing. I'll be ready."

"We'll take a drive around the interesting spots that we can still see in the twilight. Would you like to go to the Lido tomorrow evening?"

It was rather daring, but still they could see a show which featured superlative international artists. She agreed that it would be interesting.

"We'll dine at your hotel first, if that's agreeable."

Very nice, she thought as he said good night. She composed herself once more for sleep.

13

THE Paris trip was not only successful, but infinitely satisfying to Charla. She brought home a business contract for her brother's firm to supply fabric to Mlle. Mouson's house of designers for exports, as well as for a newer customer.

She had also been asked to join an international organization consisting of fashion coordinators, who worked with leathers as well as with fabrics, with shoe designers as well as with dress manufacturers.

"It gives me an excuse to fly to Paris once in a while!" she laughingly told her brother Barrett.

"Wonderful for the business, too, Sis. Gee! I'm really proud of you and this special accomplishment."

After she had gone upstairs to her room that first night back at Arden Manor, Jennie said, "I think the little holiday was especially good for her. She looked so pale for a time especially after the bicycle accident."

Charla and Jeff had had a wonderful time in Paris, she had told Barrett and Jennie. They had managed to take several historic tours, had spent some time at the Louvre, and had been able to visit Versailles. She had been entranced with the palace and the grounds, and bought several wonderful pictures and a package of slides. She now had quite a large collection of colored slides and sometimes showed them to the family.

Jeff had asked her to go riding with him the following Saturday, and she was looking forward to being on Vixen again. She had not been in the saddle since the day of the fall, and she had begun to realize that she was unconsciously shunning the opportunity by appearing to be too busy.

One night in Paris she had been unable to sleep and had finally started thinking about her brother's household, her unexpected trip to England, and the shop. Just before going to sleep, she thought that she must start riding again before she developed some sort of phobia about it. Fear was one thing she disliked cultivating. It would be absurd even to consider being afraid of Vixen; although the horse was spirited, he was also gentle.

She went out to the stable early Saturday afternoon to see if the saddle had been repaired. She'd forgotten to mention it, and she wondered if Court had had it taken care of before he left for Scout Camp. She went into the quiet tack room, saw the gear all up in place. Passing the children's saddles, she went directly to the one she had used.

The leather strap which had broken had not been repaired. She presumed it would need to be taken into a leather shop. She gave a little sigh of dismay and exasperation, picked up the loose end and ran her hand along the edge. There was a jagged tear, but she suddenly gasped. The strap had been cut almost to the center; there was no doubt about it! She could feel the difference between the cut and the tear.

She began to shake.

This had been done intentionally!

A number of other incidents which had

seemed purely accidental flashed through her mind.

Mike!

Why on earth Mike? Why would he want her to be injured?

She shrugged her shoulders. She had certainly been instrumental in his doing a better job, as far as scheduling his work and really accomplishing things went. But he couldn't possibly hold that much resentment against her.

And he couldn't have had anything to do with the big car that had nearly run her down on the road when she was bicycling home from the bus.

She would use Court's saddle this afternoon. And she would remember to ask Jeff to remove the strap and take it to the leather shop near her office.

She felt a little uneasy now around the house, and looked questioningly at Mike the next time she encountered him. He was polite as always and seemed to keep busy, mowing, clipping, weeding eternally around the place, feeding and tending the stock. Occasionally he drove her to the bus line to catch the interurban for London. At such times he always wore a uniform and was very courteous.

There was an early feeling of fall late in August, and all the days which could be spent outdoors became even dearer to Charla, as she realized that next year at this time she would probably be back at her old job in San Francisco.

She and Jeff spent longer afternoons on the weekends riding, and sometimes playing a set of tennis. She swam rather well, and sometimes they took a picnic dinner down to the river on the far side of the Arden estate. They often went boating and sometimes hiked to the top of the hill and just sat and enjoyed chatting and looking at the scenery.

She found Jeff, like many Englishmen, liked to read, and they discussed some of the world's best literature, Charla really feeling as though she needed a refresher course.

On the first day of September Barrett suddenly looked up from his desk where he was checking a folder she'd brought home from the office. "You know, I've just realized that your six months' leave is just about up, Charla, and I'm not ready to let you go back."

"And I've been so busy I've not even thought of it lately. But you know, Barrett, when I was in Paris I began to feel if you wanted me to stay longer, there's no real reason I shouldn't."

"You've been a lifesaver for me. I think you know that. Jennie and I are so grateful."

"I'm glad that it's been a help. I've really enjoyed it, and lately, especially since I went to Paris, I feel that maybe I'm earning a little of my salary!"

Barrett nodded. "The only thing is that it's really not enough. And, too, if you think that you'd rather stay in London part of the time, you could get an apartment. It would make it easier for you. I don't know what we'd do without you here, though. You're good for all of us; it keeps things so much more cheerful!"

"Oh, I would want to stay on here; if the weather gets too bad, occasionally I might stay overnight in a hotel."

Jennie, bustling in with hot milk for Barrett, was greeted with, "Great news, honey! I've talked Charla into staying with us longer. We can't afford to let her go from the shop just yet."

A pleased smile broke over Jennie's face. "Just so we don't impose on you, Charlotte. Barrett's a little selfish; I think we all are, as far as you're concerned. You've been so wonderful for all of us. Besides, there's Jeff. He'll not let you go so easily."

Charla blushed. Yes, there was Jeff. In spite of an occasional kiss, Jeff was still a little reserved with her. She knew there must have been another girl or so in his life before she'd met him. Yet he'd only mentioned one, Alice Lindsey, a very popular girl who lived in Sussex. The mention had been casual, and Charla was almost certain that Jeff was not serious about her.

"What about your young man back in San Francisco?"

"Greg Vincent is not one to wait very long for a gal. I think he's enjoying life as usual; there are lots of really pretty girls there, and I don't think he's missed me, too much!"

"Don't belittle your charms!" said Barrett. "I hope we've not broken anything up, Sis."

"Indeed not!" she said lightly. "In fact, I was glad to get away to think things over. I'm rather sure he's not the kind of man I'd like to marry."

They mentioned Court and Judith, who would be coming home soon now and getting ready for school. This term Court was being sent to a boarding school, and it would be Judith's last year at the Academy. Next year she'd be going to a famous girls' school, but that was still too far away to give much thought to. She, like Court, had been enrolled since early childhood.

"I've so much sewing to look after. I must get Miss Beakley to come next week, just as soon as Judith gets home. There will be hems to let down, at least two new tweed skirts for her, and those dreadful uniforms must be ready."

"Actually, in some ways they're a blessing. You don't have to worry so much about new styles for girls, and at her age it can become an obsession!"

They spoke of the new fall fabrics and the exhibition of new highland tweeds and some of the beautiful shetland woolens that were coming into the shop.

"Silks will pick up again in November, for the Christmas trade, especially in America. Every girl practically has to have a new print for the holiday season."

Charla recalled seeing the beautiful woolens being lined up in the special showrooms. Missing from some of the largest tables were the silks, especially the light, airy designs. The heavy failles, ottomans, the damasks for cocktails and dancing were of course available. A bit later the lovely new chiffons and other sheers for floating, long-skirted evening dresses would be popular. Actually the world of fabrics was an exciting one. She would be called in for consultation on buying some of the new patterns from now on. Mrs. Tomlinson might not appreciate it, but Barrett had assured Charla that her Paris success proved her to be capable along that line.

She wrote a short letter to her boss back at her old job in San Francisco, asking to be released from her promise to return at the end of her six months' leave. Actually, he had suggested that she take the leave, so as to see if she liked the work. It had been a sort of insurance policy for her, in case she wished to return. Her brother had really given her a promotion.

"You have earned yourself a very big place at the shop, Sis, and you may stay as long as you care to. I talked to Hugh Craigie about your work in his office. He pretended that he'd be able to find another girl from the employment agency if you have to give up his office work, but I could tell he would like you to stay with him."

"Barrett told him that someone else can take dictation, and that he'd prefer to trust you with some of the newer French customers!" laughed Jennie.

"I'll stay on in his office a few hours a day, breaking in the new girl," Charla had said. "I can keep up with the extra duties for a week or so."

It was going to be a little more pleasant at the shop now, she told herself, going into the city the next day. Bonnie was delighted with the new plans and Marty agreed that it was about time that someone from the family had a chance to find out first a little more about Mrs. Tomlinson's attitude.

She drives some of our best customers away, I'm sure. She has no modern ideas at all, thought Charla.

The older woman's brusqueness, her opinions given so curtly might be detrimental to the shop. Poor old Mr. Maleky was not as alert as he should be, but he did a surprising amount of work.

14

CHARLOTTE had never really felt as relaxed in Mr. Craigie's office as she'd thought she should have, after he had practically accused her of eavesdropping.

He seemed very busy most of the time. He and Mr. Maleky were in conference nearly every day.

Because of the tension that had been created between them, she was doubly glad of her new assignment. She was given the opportunity to deal with some of the London designers now, and since it was suit time, she met with one or two customers almost every day.

She was pleased that Mr. Craigie continued to work with the manufacturers of men's clothing, and that she was given more and more of the assignments to discuss women's suits.

The older, seasoned veterans from the factories came to go over contracts with her. She felt that they were a little surprised to see how young she was, but that they appreciated the colors and weaves suggested for certain styles they'd purchased from the designers.

Tea at Grosvenor House became at once a social event and a business convenience; she saw Iris Carey there once or twice in early September. Jeff asked her to stay over for the opening of Noel Coward's new play, and they made an evening of it, dining after the final curtain. Her circle of friends had begun to enlarge as she met young Lady Chenowith and one or two other of Iris' wealthier friends.

Now that the children were home for a few days before leaving for their school term, the house rang with their shouts and laughter. Both had come from their summer camps with tanned skins and, as Jennie said, bulging biceps and at least an inch taller.

Courtney didn't mention the mending of the broken saddle strap to Charlotte, and she was grateful that it was forgotten. She had never told anyone that it looked as though it had been cut, for she was fearful that it might worry her brother and Jennie.

Court and Judith had bought her a scrapbook at the local stationer's, and she had begun to paste in a few postcards and mementos from her travels. There were snaps now of most of the family. She had never taken a picture of Barrett in his wheel chair, hoping that soon he would be able to get around better with the artificial limb.

The first fitting had been unsuccessful, and Barrett was depressed for several days. The second time the doctor had prepared the family for the possibility that Barrett might balk again, but this time he had evidently made up his mind to accept the leg, and to their relief was beginning to take a few steps.

There was a picture of the whole Carey family and a very good view or two of the Carey gardens. Jeff's mother sent over a photograph of both Jennie and Charla at the tea table during the festive garden party. Charla looked lovely, and very much at home behind the big silver pot, smiling at the cluster of guests.

Surprising how much at home all of

this makes me feel now, Charla thought. She really hadn't been too homesick for San Francisco, though at first she had missed the deep-throated foghorns and the cry of the gulls above the great city on the Pacific. Greg was impatient with her. This surprised her very much. She had written him about a week after her decision to stay on in London had been made.

"I wish you'd come back. I miss you like the devil. We only loaned you to your brother's shop for six months, and now they're keeping you! We can't let that happen. Either you come over here, or I'll be coming over there to get you!"

So far there had not been a follow-up to that threat, but perhaps that was because she'd not yet answered it. Too much was going on. Her days were filled and running over.

Early in September Jeff called one evening and suggested that she ride into London with him in the mornings whenever he was going directly there, for now they would be having showers occasionally. Often, possibly two or even three days a week, he stayed at Abingdale, but at that, she would be welcome to ride that far before taking a bus on into the city.

It proved to be very helpful not only to her, but also to Jennie, who often liked to have the car, now that Barrett was feeling like getting out occasionally. Sometimes they went for long rides over the countryside, taking their lunches down to the river on sunny days, and visiting old friends such as the Careys.

One evening Charla and Jeff stayed over to see a musicale at her Majesty's Theatre. There was a light mystery connected with it, and Charla and Jeff discussed it during dinner at Simpson's afterward.

"You know, Jeff, I couldn't help noticing the parallel between the plot there and my own little special plot."

"What do you mean, Charla?" Jeff asked in amusement. "Don't tell me you have a mystery in your life."

She nodded and smiled. "It's so trivial that I've never mentioned it to either Barrett or Jennie. Just one more item for them to worry about."

"Let me be the judge. I might see a few legal aspects!"

She sketched the story of the bolt of fabric, described the Dior blue background and the white camellia print, the beauty of the material, and how she'd thought of this particular silk for a dress. Then she told of the disappearance of the two bolts of material — or of the same bolt twice. She hesitated to speak of Mr. Craigie's displeasure about the 'eavesdropping' episode, but feeling relaxed with Jeff, told it in a gay, disarming manner.

Jeff frowned thoughtfully. "I can't see how he'd think you were eavesdropping, since you had a perfect right to come into the office on a business matter, and simply overheard the reference to it."

"That's just what I can't see — what difference it made, and yet it must have been important. He pretended that the whole thing was too little for him to be bothered with later when I told him I'd like a length cut off the fabric. Just shrugged it off."

"It doesn't add up. He was too busy

to listen to your story, yet was miffed with you for overhearing a reference to the material?"

"That's right. The incongruity was the thing which caused me to think about it! But I put it out of my mind as soon as possible."

"And rightly so, too."

She blushed, thinking, it must seem petty. Men don't like such trifles. It must have been my fault. She said, "Now, back to that play again."

"Just a moment; not quite so fast. How long has Mr. Craigie been with the firm?"

"I'm not sure. Mr. Maleky was the manager for many, many years. Forty years with the firm, but in the larger capacity for at least ten, probably."

"I see." Jeff lit a cigarette and blew a smoke ring thoughtfully. "Oh, well, it's a little disturbing to lose a secretary and then to have the boss' sister in one's office, I presume."

He signed the waiter's check and then added suddenly, "Has there been anything else, no matter how small, that has bothered you since your arrival?"

She had never mentioned the near-crash of the car which she was certain had held Mrs. Tomlinson. Should she? Everything was going so well now at the shop. Of course, anyone could tell that Mrs. Tomlinson didn't like her. Did she really like anyone?

"Anything at all, Charla? Any little accident or near-accident? I know about the bicycle and Mike's cart, but there couldn't be any connection there, of course."

"Oh, absolutely not," she agreed with him. She hesitated, then added, "Oh, there was almost an accident on the road one afternoon, when I was going home from the bus station, on my bike. A car appeared suddenly around a curve, then shot across my path. I almost struck it. Rather, it almost ran me down. But I was confused. I was so new, at the beginning of my stay here, and unaccustomed to see cars on that side of the road, so I considered it might be my own fault."

"And how about it now? Do you still feel that way?"

"I just don't know. You see I had the

oddest feeling. After I got my bearings again, I realized that I had recognized a woman in the car. At least I *thought* I did. I've never told anyone, Jeff. And I dislike doing so now."

Jeff leaned forward anxiously. "Who was it, Charla? You must tell me, even if you only *think* you might have recognized her. Who was it?"

"Mrs. Tomlinson, who works in the shop."

"But wouldn't it be impossible for her to be there at that time, if she left the shop at the same time you did?" Jeff asked. Then he answered his own question. "Of course she could have been. A car would go right through, whereas a bus has a lot of stops to make. But why? Why would she want to run you down?"

"I'm sure I don't know. It's silly to attach any importance at all to the fact that she was cross about the disappearance of the fabric that first time. She just waved it aside; you recall I said that she pretended or rather acted as though I'd been mistaken in the color. She might have convinced me later, if I hadn't seen the same print that second time."

He nodded. "It must be confusing to see thousands of bolts of materials, all the colors of the rainbows and shades between. Are you sure?" He laughed shortly. "What a question to ask a woman. Of course you're certain!"

He helped her with her fur cape. "Try to remain fairly relaxed, but keep your eyes open. If anything unusual happens, let me know at once."

She realized later that she'd not mentioned the cutting of the leather strap on her saddle which had caused her fall from Vixen. How could that have had any connection with the incidents which had occurred at the shop?

15

THE social season in London opened with the first cool days and the whole great city seemed to gather itself for an onrush of fall activities. It was apparent in the rush for new fashions and the upsurge of sales in the woolens department. Arden, Limited became much more active and summer lethargy dropped quickly into the past as the momentum increased. Each day brought new interests and some problems.

One day late in September Charla had a cable from Greg Vincent in San Francisco. At last he was carrying out his threat to 'come and get her.'

He did not really ask permission to come see her. He simply stated the time of his arrival at the London airport. Naturally he hoped she would meet him. However, the time was not convenient, and after all, she lived at a place near a village, several miles from the nearest bus station. He would stay at the Abingdale Arms the first day or so. Reading the words, Charla felt sudden dismay. He evidently planned to stay for some time in England. She knew that he'd never been in Europe and presumed that this would be his annual vacation, of perhaps two weeks possibly longer.

Unless he rented a car, it would be quite inconvenient to get to Arden Manor, and the hours would be difficult. He must pay for having taken it for granted that she would be able to spend much time with him. Within ten days she had some very important meetings and was preparing some material in advance for them. A bit angry, she wrote a cablegram herself and sent it, hoping that it would reach him before he left.

It didn't sound very hospitable. "Sorry I'm going to be very busy at the office this next two weeks. Can you postpone your trip?"

The only answer she had was his telephone call from the Abingdale Arms two days later.

In the meantime Barrett and Jennie had assured Charla that she simply must ask him to come stay at Arden Manor. "The least we can do, dear, is to help entertain your young American friend. I wouldn't think of having him spend his stay at the Arms!"

"But he doesn't expect to stay with us. Americans are used to hotels. Besides, he didn't have any right just to wire me that he was coming without first seeing if he was wanted!"

Jennie had no immediate reply, but later insisted that if Charla wished, that she invite Greg to come to the house. Barrett was less insistent.

"Actually, it sounds to me as though Charla doesn't really want him to come. Leave it to her, Jennie. She'll do the right thing, and perhaps it would be better if he isn't here with us. I agree that he should have had permission to come first!"

Charla had a little difficulty explaining to Jeff why she couldn't stay over to see a play for which he'd already bought the tickets and reserved seats.

"He'll arrive here that very day. Oh, Jeff, I'm sorry, but I just can't go with you."

164

"I don't see why not. After all, let him sit around and wait for you, and learn that he can't do anything he wishes without consultation." Jeff was unusually miffed.

"It might be a good thing for him to twiddle his thumbs all evening as penance for taking me for granted." She laughed.

"Good! Serve the inconsiderate pup just right, too."

"Let me think about it, and I'll tell you for sure on the way into town tomorrow." Charla added, "The more I think about it, the more I feel all of you are right. Of course my sister-in-law feels we should be more hospitable, but that's because she thinks he's such a good friend."

"And isn't he?"

"Not that good." She was remembering other times when Greg Vincent had taken her for granted. Several times he had called just before seven in the evening for dates. Once she was certain it was because another girl had broken one with him. But tonight, here in England, all of that seemed very far away. And Greg's arrival seemed inexplicably unreal.

She did go to the play with Jeff, after having left a message at the Abingdale Arms for Greg. It was a cool greeting for one who had traveled thousands of miles to see her, yet it keynoted her feeling for him. He had ignored her cabled answer to his announcement that he was coming, so he couldn't expect her to drop everything to meet him.

His call was waiting for her when she went into the house that evening after Jeff escorted her to the door. To be sure she wouldn't miss it, Jennie was waiting up for her.

"Molly took the first call, and simply told him that you weren't in. Luckily I answered his second. He left a message for you to call him, no matter how late."

Charla, waiting for the call to go through, wondered how she could greet him. However, all of that was taken care of. He still took her for granted!

"Darling! I'm so sorry you were tied up with an old poky meeting and we couldn't get together this evening. Now, I have everything planned for tomorrow. I've a nice little English Ford for my stay here. I'll come out and pick you up about nine in the morning, and we'll do this lovely countryside, have tea and lunch at some old inn and then dinner in London."

"Oh, Greg." She was trying to think fast. How could she not spend the day with him? It would be unforgivable to pretend that she couldn't take a single day, especially when the shop belonged to her brother.

"I won't take *no* for an answer. I'm very anxious to see you, and we have so much to talk about." All of the old warm undertones were in his voice. Like a magnet, she was drawn to him.

She was suddenly almost afraid to see him.

"I'll call my office and say I won't be there tomorrow," she said. "But, Greg, I cabled that this is an especially busy season, and I won't be able to take very much time off."

"Come now, Darling. Your brother's no slave driver! It's time you had a few days off. I'll bet that you've worked every day since your arrival, now haven't you?"

"Why, yes, of course. I was so badly needed. And the situation hasn't changed. In fact, I've had quite a promotion and am buried in work. You've no idea . . . "

"Let's not talk about it now, Charla."

Of course, Greg never wanted to talk about work! But then, of course, Jeff wasn't like him. Imagine Greg going to a fashion show with her!

"I'll see you at nine in the morning," Greg was saying.

She replaced the receiver on its hook with mixed emotions. She wanted to see Greg, and still she felt impatient with him.

She had to cancel two appointments for the next day. It did not please her, but both of the men were quite nice about it and postponed the meetings until the day after.

She ate a late breakfast from a tray in her room, brought in by Kit.

"Is your toast good and hot, miss? I'll be glad to get some other if it's cooled. That Mike stopped me for a minute on the way. He's washing windows today."

"It's just fine Kit." Charla wanted to

ask about Mike and also how Kit's romance with him was coming along, but she dropped the thought immediately. "Leave my room cleaning until a bit later this morning, will you, please?"

"Oh, yes, miss."

The girl seeemd more anxious to please the whole family of late, and even Molly had had some good words for her during the past few weeks. Jennie had said that Mike and Kitty were still going down to the village cinema at least once a week, and that he spent one evening with Kit, just walking on the country roads and going into the village occasionally on special errands in the car. He had not been at the local pub so much lately, and was doing very well on the grounds and seemed to be getting excellent results from the vegetable garden.

Of course, Charla thought, the bike and barrow collision could have been pure accident. She seldom let herself think of the cut leather strap, for that was too frightening. Mike would be the only member of the household who would have access to the tack room, though, without arousing suspicion.

Right now everything was going along so smoothly at the shop that there could be no cause for suspicion or alarm in any of the departments. Later, she was certain, Mrs. Tomlinson would be replaced by her brother when he was able to return to his shop. It was apparent that she was not the kind of person needed in that position. Eventually Mr. Maleky would reach his retirement age and just naturally leave, and from then on the draper's should prove to be quite successful, bringing in more than an adequate income.

She dressed in a warm brown tweed suit, adding brown leather pumps with stacked heels, a pert brown hat with a bit of fur at the right side; a symphony in browns, symbolic of fall.

Jennie smiled at her in the hall before she went downstairs, saying, "You look perfectly precious! He won't be able to resist you in that costume."

"Maybe I should change, then. I do feel a little resistant myself. Oh, Jennie, what's the matter with me? I'm not the least excited about Greg's coming all the way over here."

"Wait until you see him. Maybe then you'll know the answer or at least feel differently. There must be more than just a slight acquaintance between you, or he'd not have flown all the way from San Francisco."

"I know. I was glad to get away last April so that I could think things over. We were approaching the engagement stage."

"It would make us very happy if you stayed in England the rest of your life." Jennie put an affectionate arm around her. "Oh, Charla, you'll never know what it's meant to us to have you here!"

Charla kissed her warmly. "I've never been happier than with all of you." She heard the chimes at the front door. "There's Greg. I'll let Molly open the door." She felt a little flurry of excitement at last. In a moment she would be seeing him after almost seven months.

She heard his voice asking for her. Molly's reply floated up the stairs as she led him to the drawing room. Charla waved a hand toward her sister-in-law and went downstairs. The great house was quiet. She could hear the whirr of the mower in the distance where Mike was cutting grass, and a faint chirping of birds in the wood. Her heels were quiet on the heavily carpeted stairs.

Greg was lighting a cigarette as she came into the room. He laid it down, springing to his feet and holding out both hands to catch her shoulders and to pull her toward him for a kiss.

It was a long kiss, and then he held her away from him and searched her face eagerly. "You've changed a little. You're prettier than ever, if that's possible. Oh, Charla, I've missed you." He started to kiss her again, but this time she drew back a little.

"You're browner, Greg. You must have played a lot of golf and swum a lot, haven't you?"

He nodded. "I had a good summer, except that I missed you like the very devil. Oh, Charla, isn't it time you came back home?"

She shook her head. "No, not now, Greg. I can't possibly come very soon — if I do at all, that is. I'm doing some very important work for my brother; it's a special coordinating job that I personally started for him while in Paris."

He picked up his cigarette. His hand shook a little while he lit it. "The indispensable woman?"

"Laugh if you wish. It sounds ridiculous to a man who sees people replaced daily in a great city like San Francisco, but this is a little different. After it's a going project someone else is welcome to take it over, but right now it's my pet."

He smiled tolerantly. "I can't blame you. One does like to see something he's initiated succeed. Shall we get started on our excursion? I want you to show me the sights around this area. In the meantime," he said smoothly, "I may be able to convince you that you're needed back home."

16

NOW and then she stole a look at Greg as they traveled over the road. Traffic was not heavy. The morning office-goers and shop-bound personnel had left earlier, and this was certainly the off-season for tourists, so they met only an occasional farmer or housewife going into the nearby villages on errands.

It was a beautiful fall day, heady with the snap of coolness yet filled with sunshine. Heavy dew stood up on vines and in the shrubbery along the wayside, and the grasses stood browned and the fields idle after the haying. Occasionally the river was seen in the distance, sparkling but placid, and now and then a boat or small passenger vessel was observed as they made their way downstream toward the next town.

The names were entrancing even yet to Charla, and she repeated them aloud from time to time. They followed the course of the Thames as much as possible, passing through Warbrough, Shillingford, Whitchurch, Reading, Caversham, Marlow, Burnham, Twickenham, and Teddington. They ate lunch at Henley-On-The-Thames and took time to select a few trinkets for the girls in Greg's office. There was a table of ceramics and some silver spoons bearing the names of Henley and the great schools, Oxford and Cambridge.

"How to be very, very popular," Charla said, smiling as she helped him put the gift-wrapped packages in the car.

"And how to have to pay overweight on my flight home." Greg grinned. "Of course, I can gather it all up and get it mailed directly from London, which I'll do if it gets to be too much of a good thing."

"Don't forget you can buy five hundred dollars worth of goods without paying duty if you stay long enough."

"How long is long enough? Time to convince you to go back with me, Charla?"

She merely smiled, shaking her head. They left the car at one place and went on board a pleasure craft and rode several miles down-river before returning to the locks where they'd embarked. Only a few other passengers were on board; they had most of the deck to themselves.

Greg talked only a little of his work. He had had one promotion since she had left and was being sent to New York in December to attend a national convention. He would be expected to bring back information to his co-workers.

"Maybe you could meet me there if you don't come back sooner. Christmas in Manhattan — wouldn't that be exciting?"

But Charla was thinking of Christmas in San Francisco, of the wonderful, old days when her parents were living and later, of the house of her aged aunt up on Russian Hill. Her thoughts flitted without warning to Arden Manor, and then, curiously, to Jeff Carey's home. She could almost see the traditional holidays as enacted at Carey Hall. She could see herself present with Jeff, Iris and the older Careys.

"What are you thinking about, Charla? You're a million miles away. Was it last year's office party?"

She laughed. "Oh, no! Something much more serious than that could possibly be! Oh, look, Greg, see those lovely wild birds over there in the trees?" Anything to get him off the subject, before she had to confess her own thoughts.

In the mid-afternoon they took a Salter's steamer over another delightful stretch of the river, journeying upstream to Oxford. They enjoyed the ever-changing scene, from lush green meadows to tree-clad hills. Before reaching Sandford Lock, they passed Nuneham House. In this park, they could plainly see the carved initial of the conduit which had once stood in the center of Oxford, and its two tanks holding water which had been fit for drinking when most city wells were foul and plague-ridden. Charles II had filled the tanks with wine — at least they had been so filled for his coronation!

Leaving Iffley Lock, they entered the stream known by Oxford men as the 'Gut' and saw suddenly the few unspoiled remaining spires of Oxford. Later on, they passed Chaucer's house in Woodstock, and thence to Blenheim Palace. Here,

Charla repeated the tale of the Fair Rosamond and the romance connected with her and Henry II. The great house, home of Winston Churchill and the earlier house of Marlborough, seemed only of slight consequence to Greg, and Charla felt impatient with him and lapsed into a long silence. It was broken by Greg when he said, "You don't really go for all of this royalty business, do you?"

Having watched the devotion of the Britons to their Queen for the past several months, she could not take it so lightly.

"Even though it isn't our way of life," she defended, "I accept it and respect it as the tradition of millions of people who have great love for their country. Besides, I like history, and the romance of the early days of any country."

"Okay, okay!" Greg laughed. "So it isn't as exciting as baseball or the fights! Just a difference of opinion, honey. Say, maybe I *had* better take you back to your home base. You're not falling in love with this country, are you?" There was a serious note in his voice.

"I could, easily enough. It's fascinating. Besides, remember that my brother and his family live here. There are many things about England that I like very, very much."

"Don't let that influence your relationship with any young males. Now, don't you think it's time that you told me a little more about this Carey fellow? You're not serious about him, are you?"

She resented the question. After hesitating a brief instant, she said defiantly, "Enough so that I wouldn't break a date with him last night so that I could meet you, Greg. It wasn't cricket."

"Cricket!" Greg laughed. "You've even started talking like them. Gad, woman, I'll have to get you away from here." He lit a cigarette; the eternal way of showing his utter calm. "So you are serious about him?"

"I've not really thought about it, Greg."

Isn't that a little white lie? Weren't you thinking about Christmas at Carey Hall just a little while ago?

"Oh, well, if he's not made enough of an impression for you to think seriously about him, after all these months, then

I don't believe I've anything to worry about."

The toot of the returning steamer signaled them, and they went back aboard. It was a quiet, peaceful journey back to the starting place, and she wished she'd spoken a little less sharply to Greg.

They drove back to Arden Manor about dusk, and she took him into the house and to the sitting room where her brother and his wife were listening to the early news. After introductions, she went upstairs to change into a dinner dress, for they were going to eat at the King's Arms, a traditional roast beef place where many Londoners dined fashionably in the evenings in the winter. They would stop by Greg's hotel where he, too, could change into evening clothes.

There was a small vase of bright red rosebuds on her dressing table and a note which read, *"Remember me, Jeff."*

She stood there a moment, holding the roses close and drinking in their fragrance. She could picture Jeff, tall, serene, his eyes studying her seriously.

She could feel the touch of his hand on her arm, and the feel of his lips against her own.

She picked up her phone and called his number, waited breathlessly for his voice. "Jeff, it's me, I mean I. Thank you for your lovely flowers. I am remembering you."

"See that you do, Charla, dear," he said playfully. "I just thought I'd send you the reminder. And how about lunch tomorrow? You will be going to your office, won't you?"

"Yes, to both questions. Lunch and the office. What time, Jeff?"

"About one?"

It was agreed, and she put back the receiver almost with a sense of guilt. Let Greg ask about her day, and she could tell him that tomorrow was completely filled.

She would recommend the National Gallery and the British Museum, maybe the Wallace Collection! And if he needed more, perhaps he could go to a tailor's on Bond Street, or visit the Wax Works! She slipped a little booklet in her purse, 'London Social Events.' That should give him some information on things to do and places to eat.

Jennie came upstairs before Charla was ready to go out.

"He's really quite handsome, dear. And I can tell that Barrett likes him. He's a little brusque, after hearing the businessmen of our country all these years, but he does have a way with him, doesn't he?"

"Decidedly so," agreed Charla. Of course Greg had a way with him. The old charm. It had begun to work on her several times today. But then, he had offended her several times today, too. And she had kept thinking about Jeff, comparing the two men.

"And do I look all right to go out with that charming American?"

She turned around for inspection. The low cut black chiffon gown was beautiful. She had worn it twice for Jeff, so she didn't mind using it tonight. Her lovely white throat was bare, but her earrings flashed fire, and there was a wide bracelet on her right arm. She pulled on white gloves, gave her sister-in-law a quick kiss and picked up her mink stole.

"You look — what's the American word — scrumptious!"

"You are a very satisfactory sister, you know, Jennie," said Charla. "Thanks, too, for putting my roses in water for me. I called Jeff."

"That was thoughtful, Charla. We do admire Jeff, you know."

"Yes, I know." Admire was an inadequate word. She knew how they really felt about Jeff. But they'd never push him!

Her brother and Greg were deep in men's talk about business and the trends, the Summit meeting and the elections. Politics, the Soviet Union, Cuba and the Congo had no doubt been taken care of, Charla thought.

"Got everything settled?" she asked lightly, laying her hand on Barrett's sleeve.

He grinned. "As much as some others are likely to in the same amount of time. Going now?"

"Expect we'd better get started. I have to change yet." Greg picked up his light topcoat and hat. "It's great to get to meet you, Mr. Gordon, after all these years."

"A pleasure. Now, count on us for a dinner or two while you're here."

Greg nodded. "Thanks. I hope it's all right with Charla. We almost came to blows a time or two today. I think she's being brain-washed!" He spoke lightly, but she knew that he was intimating that she'd lost her love for her country, and she resented that more than anything she'd heard him say today.

"We'll battle that one out on the way to dinner, Greg!"

And battle it out they did, from the time they stepped into the little car until they reached the hotel. Charla spoke in definite, glowing terms of her feeling toward America in general and San Francisco in particular.

"Which leaves me exactly no leg to stand on," said Greg. "I'm yelling 'Uncle' and I retract anything I've even implied. You are here only for the purpose of helping out your brother and forwarding a project that, once started, must be carried on until it's a routine procedure. Okay, Charla, I know when I'm bested. Now let's forget it and have a wonderful evening on the town, though I doubt you could paint the King's Arms anything like a shade of red!"

She laughed. It was impossible to be angry for long with Greg. "Only a reasonable facsimile!" she admitted. "But we'll try. Oh, Greg, be patient with me. I'll be back in no time in San Francisco, and then you'll be sorry you came and reminded me to be homesick. Actually, it wasn't all beer and skittles the first month, believe me. I missed the old bellering fog horns and the lovely misty-moisty fog like everything. But in April, we had some real fog ourselves over here."

"Then you're not mad at me, honey?"

"Of course not. You're just the same, Greg. You haven't changed one little iota."

He was suddenly very serious. "Oh, yes, I have, Charla. I know that I love you." The lights of the village suddenly sprang up from around the final curve in the road. He turned the car deftly, and they came up to a broad parking area. He turned off the motor and then caught up her hand. "Charla, marry me. I came all the way over here to see you once more and to know for sure that it wasn't the distance. Marry me, Charla?"

She had known all along that he would ask the quesiton.

And she had also known that she wouldn't be quite ready to answer it.

17

CHARLA slept very little that night. She rose about two o'clock and, going to her window, sat looking out at the bright moonlit gardens, the lawns, boxed in neatly with hedges, and fancied that she could even catch a glimpse of the Thames in the distance.

Her evening with Greg after his direct proposal had been most disturbing. She knew that last winter he had been on the point of asking her to marry him more than once, but she had avoided it neatly. She realized now the real reason for her uneasiness about his coming to England. She had anticipated this proposal.

She heard the sound of the great clock in the downstairs hall, softly chiming the hour of three, and shuddered at the thought of an early rising to make the bus at Kingston.

Greg was fairly reasonable about not seeing her the next day until dinner time. He said that he would bow his back and take in some of the tourists' sights; one really must do certain expected things when in London. You really couldn't decently return to the States without having seen the Changing of the Guard, Parliament Buildings, Trafalgar Square, the Old Curiosity Shop, the Tower and the Crown Jewels, not to mention hearing Evensong at the Abbey, walking in the great parks, shopping at Harrod's, and all the many things they'd spoken of back in San Francisco at his office.

His office friends had surprised him with two tickets in the stalls for the current hit at Her Majesty's Theatre, and he must see some of the races at Epsom Downs. A tennis match, a jousting tournament, the gardens at Kew and some of the great manor houses were on his schedule, and in a way Charla was quite relieved. His days would be filled.

Charla managed to fall to sleep at daylight, and was groggy when her sister-in-law tapped on her door at seven.

"If I don't get up and take a cool bath, I'll never be able to make it this morning."

"Honey, Jeff just called and said he'll

pick you up at eight, unless you call him back."

"Isn't that wonderful. Just like him, too." Appreciation for his thoughtfulness quite overcame her. Jennie offered her a cup of coffee, pouring it from the lovely silver pot on a tray.

Charla drank it gratefully. "Tell Kit to bring my tray up in about thirty minutes, please, and I'll be ready if it kills me!" She slid her slender feet into satin mules. "I just couldn't seem to get to sleep, Jennie. You're a dear to bring me the plasma!"

Jennie laughed. "It must have been quite an evening."

"And after a whole day out in the open, too. After all that fresh air it's a wonder I didn't fall asleep at the dinner table!"

"Why don't you stay home today?" asked Jennie.

"Appointments, postponed from yesterday. No, sir. I'm a career girl, and I love it. I'll be okay, honey. Tell Molly no egg this morning; just juice and toast and more coffee, please."

Somehow she was ready when Jeff

pulled up in the drive for her, and in spite of her restless night, Charla looked quite fit and felt ready for the day.

It passed by swiftly. The appointments in the morning added up to a pleasant surprise in the form of two new contracts to furnish fabrics for a whole new line of wool suits to two different companies. Charla knew that her brother would be very pleased. Even Mr. Craigie gave her a glowing compliment, and this made her day complete. Jeff and she met for lunch at Grosvenor House, and there she was happy to see Iris who dropped in for a moment to say hello to her brother whom she'd not seen for two weeks.

"I'm off to Switzerland, Jeff, and won't be home for about a week, but do tell Mums that I'll call her tomorrow."

"Promise now, and be sure that you do," he admonished her.

Iris flashed a quick smile at Charla. "See how bossy he is? They get worse as they get older, too."

"I thought Dad was fairly mellow, seeing as how he bought you that new Mercedez Benz," chided her brother.

Iris smiled with delight. "Want to

borrow it sometime, Greg? It'll open your eyes."

He nodded. "I could bet on that! No, thanks, I'll just stay with my little car. Serves me very well."

There is nice camaraderie between them, Charla thought. And there did seem to be enough money for Iris to have almost anything her heart desired.

On the way back to Charla's office, Jeff asked her to have dinner with him. She explained that Greg had tickets for a play, and she could see no way out of going with him.

"How long will he spend in London and vicinity?"

"I'm not really sure. Jeff, I do want you to meet him."

"Of course I must. How about my taking the two of you to dinner later in the week?"

She agreed that it might be possible, and said that she'd ask Greg. "I'm not planning on being with him every night, believe me. I have some folders to study, and I'm also helping make up some copy for a national ad to place in some of the American magazines. I cabled him that it was a very busy time for me, and I do hope he won't expect too much attention."

During the afternoon it was a little difficult to keep her mind on her work, as it had been a very exciting day.

She had agreed that Greg should pick her up about five and drive her home from the office. They had a cocktail at a fashionable place in Abingdale before dinner.

The play was very good and she was glad to go home directly afterward. "A girl must think of her career, you know," she insisted when Greg wanted to come in the house.

They fell into a sort of schedule through necessity. He roamed the city, even went on a tour to Cambridge and one to Canterbury to broaden his knowledge of English literature, and for the historical background.

With sudden inspiration, she told him he certainly must fly up to Edinburgh and take one of the Scottish tours into Loch Lomond and the Trossacks country. To her utter amazement he complied with her suggestion.

She knew that his going only meant postponement of the reply to his proposal. She thought also of encouraging him to fly to Paris. He could fly over one morning and back the next night, thus being able to take in several night clubs, the tour to Versailles and the other historical tours which she herself had enjoyed.

Just before he left for Scotland, he made reservations for the Paris trip, although he seemed very disappointed that Charla could not accompany him.

"Not even if I wait until the weekend?"

"Especially not if you wait for the weekend. Go when I can't spend any time with you."

"But Paris alone won't be nearly so much fun as it would be if you were with me."

She was thinking of all the lovely sight-seeing she had done accompanied by Jeff. It would spoil it for her, she knew, if she went back over the same grounds with anyone else.

Actually she was glad of the respite when Greg was away on the two sight-seeing jaunts. She and Jeff had dinner together the two nights that Greg was in Edinburgh, and both nights the next week when Greg was in Paris.

The evening the three of them dined together was just before Greg's departure for the States. He was to take the polar route, and his take-off time was early one morning, the second week of October. Charla decided to drive him to the airport that day, taking the little car with her, then going to her office and driving back early in the evening to Arden Manor. She simply didn't want Greg to go back home thinking she'd neglected him. She realized he resented going with Jeff for dinner two nights before he was to leave.

Jeff borrowed his sister's big car to pick both Greg and Charla up at seven o'clock. They drove directly back to London and went immediately to Claridge's.

The old traditional service, the handsome, but quiet dining room and the excellent menu selected by Jeff in advance left nothing to be desired. Yet Charla knew that Greg was comparing it with dinner at the St. Francis at San Francisco, or the Mark Hopkins.

Irrevocably he was taking Jeff's measure, too, Charla knew.

Both men were impeccably dressed, each in evening attire, handsomely groomed, so that many eyes fell upon the small dinner party of three. Charla had tried hard to get Iris to join them, but had been unsuccessful.

"Of course not, dear Charla. I think it's so amusing, almost like a Noel Coward play. The young American being looked over by your English friend to see if he's suitable for you." Iris' silvery laughter denoted her amusement.

"How can you be so discerning?" Jeff had inquired.

"It isn't easy. Actually, I would like to join you, but I have an engagement."

She had said that if it were possible, she and her date would drop into Claridge's about nine-thirty to see how the plot progressed.

So Charla was not surprised when the two were shown to their table. Iris made quite an impression on Greg. She was so lovely with her natural blondeness, her exquisite gown and her artificially demure manner.

Afterward, Charla told her brother all about it, adding that Iris had truly gone all out deliberately.

"Before they left she called young Lady Chenowith over; you recall I met her once. She had one of Margaret's friends in tow, and truly it was a little theatrical. I know that Greg was feeling a little unreal in the midst of all this sudden glory; he'll have something to talk about at the water cooler in the office."

"If I weren't so relieved, I'd think you were mercenary, Sis. I'll confess that Jennie and I've been worried that Greg would manage to take you back to San Francisco. Did he try?"

She nodded. "I still have to give him my answer — on the day he leaves."

"He proposed?"

"Yes. I knew that he would, too. I practically ran away last spring, you recall, so that I could get a new perspective."

"And did you? Or is all of this too personal?"

She leaned over his chair and kissed him. "Indeed not! After all, you're the only family I have, you know. I need to tell someone, but Jennie and I've not had a chance to have much woman talk the past few days."

"Have you made your decision?"

"I think so, Barrett. In fact, it practically made itself. I'm just not in love with Greg. I'm afraid I like San Francisco better than the man, and if I returned, it would be because of the city."

Barrett threw his head back and laughed. "What a blow that statement would be to a conceited man."

"How did you like Greg, Barrett?"

Her brother took a long moment to knock his pipe out, refill it and light it. "I'm not sure yet, Sis. I didn't exactly take to him, at least not after the first meeting. It was interesting to discuss the old home town and all of the changes in the city. But as a husband for you, I simply haven't been able to fit him into the picture. I could be wrong. I've grown conservative. But the man's a little shallow, I think."

18

AS Greg's plane left the field, Charla felt a great sense of release. It had actually been a chore to come with him to see him off, for she had been able the last evening to keep him from asking her point-blank her decision. Today, she had hoped that it would be possible to avoid it again. After he was gone she began to wonder if he knew her answer without asking and was perhaps avoiding an answer, or if he wished to give her more time to consider it.

The last thing he said was, "I'm going to see you at Christmas time in New York, now. Don't forget, Charla." His last kiss was a kiss of farewell, not the demanding, long kiss of greeting.

She drove rather slowly going back into the city, as though to get all of her thoughts properly sorted and into their proper compartments. As she neared her own office building, she began to think of today's plans and tried to recall her schedule of appointments and the letters she had to get out.

She gave a last long sigh of relief as she entered the elevator. It was like shedding a great responsibility before tackling the new. She saw the old grey wall covering with a new eye. Perhaps in the spring she could get her brother to redecorate the major rooms and even to lay new carpeting.

She felt eager to get on with her work. There was a large folder of sketches lying on her desk; they were undoubtedly from the advertising firm she had been working with. All of the last few days' impatience at having to entertain Greg fell away, and she slid into her chair with a sense of alertness that she hadn't felt for two weeks.

As though Jeff respected her need for time to sort out her emotions and to try to catch up with some of her work, he didn't call her for two days. She began to wonder if she had disappointed him on the evening they'd dined together at Claridge's.

Then his call came at her office, and

he asked to drive her home. "I spent the last two days at Henley, on a special case, and so haven't been in touch, but I am anxious to see you, Charla. Would you care to go to dinner? We can drive back to Abingdale."

She accepted and, after replacing the receiver, felt a warm glow of anticipation suffuse her. Everything was just as it had been — before Greg had come to mar her companionship with Jeff Carey. She worked past the afternoon tea time and was ready when Jeff came to the office for her.

It proved to be a very satisfactory evening. There were only one or two possible references to Greg. He might never have interrupted their schedules! Jeff brought one of the early fall social calendars and they went through the next week's interesting events, selecting a musical they wanted to see, and a Saturday afternoon boat race at Henley which he had heard discussed while there earlier this week.

The Chenowiths were having a hunt party the first of November, a weekend event, and Charla and Jeff had been invited. Magda Chenowith and her brother were friends of long standing of the Careys, so Charla knew that Iris, too, would be there. She tentatively accepted the invitation. Jeff was to call for her early on Saturday morning, and there would be a pleasant hundred mile drive to the estate with its game reservation.

The winter and its social season stretched invitingly ahead of the little office girl from San Francisco, Charla thought as she went to bed about eleven. It was good to be able to get the required sleep, too!

Her niece and nephew were home for the weekend and renewed their riding, and even had a small picnic on Sunday down by the river. The rains set in the next Monday, and the sodden world began to look a little grey through the London fog. Although the whole household forced intself to be cheerful, it was quite apparent that the weather was an influence on everyone's life.

After a fortnight of rain, drizzle, sudden gusts of hard wind and a general dampening of spirits, Charla was delighted one morning to find her desk held unusually interesting mail. Some of the samples of the fabrics were coming in for the early December trade. It would seem unusually early to many people, but the spring fashion season was just around the corner.

The lovely silks, shimmering, irridescent, glamorous in the newest prints and lovely daring new colors, lay in a heap on the polished wood while she feasted her eyes upon them.

A new green, with a kind of coppery undertone, especially appealed to her. The new red, a sort of glowing deep rose, was most appealing; already in her mind's eye she could see swirling skirts on a dance floor.

The golds, the new, delicate violets and finally a flash of blue were entrancing.

Charla stood perfectly still.

There it was again. That beautiful shade of Dior blue was repeated! The white camellias blossomed lovingly over the sample, coming to life with a certain glow.

It's beautiful, just as I thought it in the very beginning, she thought. But it does seem strange that in all of this new collection this should suddenly show up.

I don't care if it's one season old. This time I *will* have a dress length from that bolt, even though I have to cut it off myself. It would be perfect for a dance dress for New Year's, and then later I could have it shortened and add a jacket, and presto-changeo I'll have a garden party dress for the Carey's annual celebration. She had already been asked to help serve refreshments! Imagine, a whole year ahead!

She was still wearing her hat, because she'd been so excited at seeing the silks that she'd not yet bothered to hang up her cloak or to remove her hat. She reached up and had turned to go to the small coat tree when she caught the eye of Mr. Craigie. He was standing just outside her door, with its glass panel, watching her. He turned quickly as she went on to get a hanger.

She opened the door and said blithely, "Good morning, Mr. Craigie. I was just looking at the lovely new silks. I can see all kinds of party dresses and summer clothes."

"They've come in, then? I've been too busy with routine things to look. Well, I hope you enjoy them. I've letters to get off." He went briskly into his own office, and she had the feeling that he was giving her a little reprimand for taking so long to look at the materials.

"How perfectly ridiculous! That's part of my job now. How can I recommend fabrics unless I know them intimately?" She would be glad when her brother could come back to the shop.

According to his doctor, that would not be so very much longer. He had been discussing it last week one night when she came in from work. Barrett was much better at using his artificial limb, and the worst of the embarrassment was now over. Jennie's and his recent excursions into the small social world in their own community had helped him meet the ordeal of facing the people he'd known.

He was quite adept at walking and getting better on stairs, too, and there would be little chance for accidents at the shop.

Charla could hardly wait for his return,

because she wanted him to see how large the whole organization had grown since he had left his office late last winter.

For two days she went back through her files, going over some of the latest contracts and setting up a list of suggestions to make to designers on the use of the silks.

She was a little tired and had a late tea about four o'clock with Bonnie and Marty. Mrs. Tomlinson was out for the day, a fact which the two older girls seemed to relish.

"I seen those new silks which came in yesterday, just a glimpse of them, of course," said Bonnie, pouring the tea. "Here, dearie, have a sweet bun with it; it'll do you good."

"Thanks, Bonnie. I will, for I'm a little tired. It's been a rough two days, working over my old files for information which I don't always seem to find at my fingertips."

"Funny how the files get the gremlins in 'em sometimes. I always think the little green men come in at night and have a high old time mixing things up for us," said Marty. "There was that old McCallister account; you remember, Bonnie, that old blister up in Edinburgh, with the long, dour face and the thick brogue! Thought we'd never get the straight of it — "

The two girls were off on a long story, and Charla listened half-heartedly. She was getting accustomed to their little attempts at humor; their only source of conversational material was the shop and their dull home lives.

Maybe it was a long day because she wouldn't be seeing Jeff tonight, for he had flown to Paris for two days to see a client whose account he handled in London.

It was pouring rain when she left her office that evening, and she got her feet soaked while waiting for her bus. It was with a damp feeling she arrived an hour and a half late at her own station where Mike awaited her at the bus stop.

He touched his hat respectfully.

"You're drenched, miss. Would you like a hot cup of tea before going home?"

"Why, thank you, no, Mike. It's kind of you to think of it, but it'll just take a few minutes now to get home so I can change."

He held open the door for her and she climbed into the back seat, thankful for the heater.

The rain had let up a bit by the time they turned into the drive at home. The house smelled spicy on the ground floor, and she was aware that Molly and Kit must be continuing their pickling and preserving of some of the garden truck and the fruits from the small orchard.

There was a long letter from Greg.

She put it aside to read after dinner when she felt more up to it. Barrett and his wife were listening to some new records, and she joined them until dinner was called.

Tonight she spoke of the blue silk with the white camellia patterns, and her brother was quick to suggest that she give a definite order to Mrs. Tomlinson for a dress length for herself.

She decided that she would do that the very first thing in the morning tomorrow, and went to her room to read her letter.

She was still thinking about the beautiful blue silk, and, sitting down on a chaise longue, she sketched a design for the dress she hoped to have made from the silk.

She fell asleep, almost immediately upon going to bed. But at midnight she was suddenly stark, staring awake and realized that the piercing shriek that had awakened her had come from her own lips.

"What is it, Charla?" Jennie turned on her overhead lights and was beside her, holding out her hand. "Are you all right? What is it?"

Charla rubbed a hand over her white brow. She couldn't speak for a long moment. In the meantime her brother came hobbling to the door of her room. "Charla! Jennie!"

"It's nothing. Just a nightmare, I guess." Charla whispered.

After she assured them she was all right and they had gone out of her room, Charla lay quietly for a long time. Sleep did not return until almost dawn, for each time she closed her eyes, all she could see was Mrs. Tomlinson holding out a long length of the blue silk with the white camellia pattern. Her thin lips repeated the same refrain:

"You'll be sorry, Miss Gordon. You'll be sorry!"

19

BY eight o'clock the next day, Charla had decided to stay home. Her head ached fuzzily, and she believed that a long ride in the open on Vixen would help her. There was not anything especially pressing today aside from her own personal wish to have a dress length of the white camellia pattern. But this morning even that seemed undesirable.

She barely touched breakfast, but drank some hot, black coffee and tried to go back to sleep. Everything seemed ridiculously safe this morning in the light of day, and she finally slept for another hour or so.

This happened to be one of the days when Jeff hadn't planned to pick her up to take her into London, so she didn't have to call him.

By noon she rather wished she had gone into her office as usual, for after her gallop and lunch with her brother and

Jennie, she was feeling fit again. She spent some time in the afternoon catching up on some of the American magazines and writing a few letters to friends back home, something which she'd neglected of late.

Greg had asked her about Christmas in New York in his last letter, but she had no plans at the present to meet him there.

Becuase of her absence, she found mail which needed special attention upon her return the following day, and most of the morning was spent in answering letters. She had orders to make out, and definite plans to work into some of the newer customers' contracts.

She ordered two bolts of the Dior blue silk with the white camellias for the casual buyer, feeling that it would be very popular. The factory would ship it immediately, because all of the samples would be available in their stock.

However, later, when the great shipments of silks arrived from their factories, Charla discovered that only one bolt of the camellia patterns was enclosed.

Charla had given instructions to the shipping clerk to bring this particular order to her attention when it came. She now stood in the small anteroom of the main storage room with the clerk who had opened the great wooden box for her.

She knew that she was out of order in personally lifting the bolt of material and taking it inside the offices with her. It was so unprecedented that she realized the men would notice immediately.

But on the other hand, they would perhaps think tolerantly, now, isn't that just like a woman?

She had barely taken a few steps when Hugh Craigie appeared suddenly in the doorway.

"Oh, Miss Gordon, let me help you!" Then in a tone of tolerant amusement, "What on earth are you doing out here in the shipping department, of all places? This isn't your forte, exactly! I'll just take care of this."

"Oh, you see, this is some material I'd like for a dress, Mr. Craigie, and I thought I'd just take it in right now."

Disbelief shot over his face.

"You have nothing pressing at your desk, then?"

Charla was furious. How could he be so high-handed?

A searing, flaming suspicion shot through her. He really didn't want her to use this silk.

There must be a reason for this.

A sudden calm came over her.

"It's not that important; just a woman's whim, I presume. Later will be all right. I'll see it in the display room and go through the regular channels."

"That's better. Sam can bring the whole box in when he's ready. Mrs. Tomlinson will take care of the display."

The calm left her as she returned through the long corridors of the shipping department, and she was shaking when she reached her desk. She sat down quickly to compose herself. She got out a few papers so as to pretend that she was working, but she sat there numbly, trying to tie everything together.

She wanted to talk with Jeff Carey again. Actually, there was very little to go on. She decided to watch everything instead. She made plans to check the shipping room again later in the day, possibly to go through the display room on her way to lunch to see if the blue silk were on the table.

But at noon nothing had been done about the new silks. There was no sign of a table being prepared to receive them. She was too busy in the late afternoon to give it much thought, and Jeff called her about five o'clock to have cocktails with him and one of his clients.

Away from the office, the matter didn't seem too important and thus faded into the background. She went with Jeff for dinner and to an early show and was home about eleven, and went to bed and slept soundly.

The next day she thought of the blue silk the very first thing, perhaps because she was a little early and none of the other girls had arrived yet. Mr. Craigie wouldn't be in the shop today, for he was leaving for Scotland on an early plane. "Off on holiday for the weekend, and getting an early start. Going to do some shooting with a friend up near Blairgowrie. Beautiful country, Miss Gordon; you should see it sometime." Friendly words late yesterday, as though it made up for his harshness of the morning encounter.

During the morning she had a chance to go through the new table of silks which had been arranged by Mrs. Tomlinson for the casual customer to browse over.

She was not at all surprised to find that the Dior blue silk with the white camellias was not among the other silks.

What is there about that one special pattern? Why is it here and then not here? Why doesn't it ever stay in sight long enough for it to become real? It's just as though I were having some kind of silly dream about fabrics.

On Friday morning she had a chance to go through the orders which Mr. Craigie's secretary was getting ready, because there was a question that the new girl didn't quite understand about procedures. She had brought in a long list of goods being sent to a New York dress manufacturer. On the second page of the packing list Charla found the bolt of 'Dior Blue with White Camellias' listed.

However, it was not listed on the invoice.

Could it have been an oversight?

The packing order was still on Mr. Craigie's desk. This meant that the goods hadn't been sent out yet.

Masking her curiosity about the discovery, Charla helped Donna, the secretary, solve her question on handling procedures, and in so doing was able to see the original orders. Donna had not omitted the bolt from the invoice through mistake! It was not listed on the original invoice, made out in Mr. Craigie's unmistakable handwriting.

After Donna had left her office, certainly unsuspecting the wild thoughts racing through Miss Gordon's mind, Charla sat calmly for a few minutes trying to map out some kind of procedure to follow.

First, I must find the material. Is it still here? It hasn't been shipped yet, for the invoice must be packed inside. Those huge wooden boxes in which the materials are shipped always contain the itemized enclosure. She had managed to collect quite a lot of information during the past six or seven months, even if she'd not spent much time outside her own office.

Second, if I find the material, what can I do about it?

Talk to Jeff. By all means talk to Jeff.

With trembling hands she lifted the receiver. Jeff was quick to note the strain in her voice.

"Can you meet me for tea at the little tea room near here?" she asked.

"Better yet, how about an early lunch?"

She thought rapidly. If she could slip into the shipping room when the men were eating their lunch, no one would see her.

Her mind was racing. The whole thing was touchy.

The timing wasn't good. On second thought, she said, "Jeff, I'd better wait and go out with you for early afternoon tea. In the meantime something more may develop."

She thought at that moment she heard a click on the other office phone, but there were two separate wires, and she realized that no one could listen in on her conversation.

"Are you sure it's best, Charla? I think

I understand you."

"Yes, I'll call you later, say about three?"

"Yes."

It had all come to her while she was talking with him. She had to see that Sam got those shipping orders and the invoice, but the whole thing was apt to backfire if she couldn't get there between the time the box was closed and its departure for the great freighter which sailed next week.

Her plan was so risky, she needed help. It would have to come from Jeff.

She could hardly wait to talk with him, yet she had to determine if the silk was in the box.

She was afraid to go out of the building and took tea with Bonnie and Marty.

"Are you ill or something, Charla? You look ghostly." Marty searched her face anxiously. "Haven't you been sleeping well?"

"I'm fine. Just need a little more sunshine, and forgot to put on any rouge this morning," smiled Charla.

She stayed in her office on the plea of there being too much work instead of going out for lunch. When the long silence indicated the men were eating their lunches, she slipped through the office's back door and through the long corridor, knowing that the men usually went around to a small pub to enjoy their lunches.

There were only two lights on in the main shipping room, and she thought she'd not be able to find the correct box, but finally she saw it, and the huge black letters looming up three inches high on the pine cover. The name of the dress manufacturers, Martyns-Oblinskey, New York City, stared up at her.

The lid was still loose — it had not been nailed in place yet — and there was no chance that it would be until the invoice was in its right place.

Right now the invoice rested in the black leather purse she was carrying, and would until she had managed to get everything under control.

Her heart hammering, she pulled up the heavy corrugated paper, then turned back the great heavy tissues and examined the labels from the end of the bolts.

Each bolt was wrapped in heavy dust-proof covers, but she found the label: Dior Blue — White Camellias No. 492566. The correct number, which she had seen on the packing order.

She replaced the coverings and tiptoed back to the corridors. She paused to listen. Suddenly she froze.

There was a rustling sound in the aisles of the shipping room. She dared not go back. Could someone have been in there, lurking in the dim corners of the old building? Don't be silly she told herself.

Nevertheless her heart beat tumultously as she continued her path to the office. Mrs. Tomlinson was still out for lunch, probably at the little hole-in-the-wall sandwich shop which she favored, since it was conveniently next door.

The afternoon's work began. There was no sign of an outburst from Mr. Craigie's secretary before three o'clock.

Donna was still so new at certain procedures that she hadn't even missed the invoice yet. The packing slip was for the men only, just to be sure that all of the order was intact. They had completed that part of their work. Now they had only to put the invoice inside.

Charla went downstairs to meet Jeff at their set time. He took her only a short distance, and then to a new place for early tea.

He was quite thoughtful, listening intently while she told him all of the details.

"You're sure the ship doesn't leave until next week, so that we'd have the weekend to look into this?"

"Yes, I'm quite sure. The trick is to get the bolt from the box and into your car."

"And if I'm caught red-handed?"

Charla paled.

"Oh, don't look so frightened. I've a Scotland Yard man, a special friend of mine, who always comes to my rescue. I think we'll phone him right away and tell him we're bringing him some suspicious material."

They continued to discuss it. The plan was all set when they parted. He wouldn't call the police, but she must be able to get the bolt from the box and to take it through the side door after all the men had left. The watchmen would come on duty about seven, and there would be plenty of time.

Everything worked out miraculously as they had planned it. There were a few frightening moments when she thought Mrs. Tomlinson was going to stay to work late, and also when the girl, Donna, came in just before five and said that the shipping men wanted the invoice and she couldn't find it.

"Now, don't cry, Donna. It'll be staring up at you from some of your papers on Monday morning. Go on home and it'll take care of itself." She would see that it did. "I'll help you the first thing. But I have a date tonight; our family's going on the last picnic of the season. A real cook-out, for the kids are home and they wanted to eat out in the open."

She was amused at how glibly the little white lies came to her lips. Donna agreed to let the missing invoice go until Monday.

"Of course, if I have to, I can simply type it from the packing order," Donna said brightly.

"That'll be just dandy!" But it wouldn't

be necessary, if she could get the material out, and the invoice in, sometime in the next few minutes!

They worked fast. It was after six, and everyone was gone, when she let Jeff in. He came up in the elevator, and together they went through the back doors, the whole route, very quietly. With a feeling of great relief she saw Jeff place the bolt of material in the trunk of his car. She went home with him. They changed their plans slightly.

They would take it to the police tomorrow. They would need plenty of time to explain the whole situation.

"And we'll feel like great fools if there's nothing wrong with the whole thing," said Jeff grimly.

20

THE family picnic was a real success. Courtney and Judith were in high spirits, and each helped in preparing the steaks and the salads. The sunset was rare and beautiful and the food tasted delicious.

Charla was in a state of excitement, but managed to eat her share and to join in the light conversation. Jeff seemed to enjoy the evening, but left early.

"I'll come for you about ten in the morning," he whispered to Charla.

She nodded. They'd simply make it look like a museum trip or something they had to attend in Abingdale. She didn't want Barrett and his wife to know anything about this mysterious business until she and Jeff had had a chance to talk to his friend about it.

It was a little after ten when Charla went up to her room to prepare for bed. She undressed, putting on her coral-colored pajamas, laying their matching robe at the foot of her bed. She paused just before turning out her light.

Someone had dropped cigarette ashes on her polished dressing table top. There could be no mistake. She opened the drawers and found that her lingerie was rumpled slightly. Going from one piece of furniture to another, she could easily see that someone had been going through her things.

It must have been a man, for a woman would be much more clever, she thought as she noticed the attempt to cover up the untidiness caused by moving hat boxes and the search which must have taken place in the back part of the closet. One dress had fallen from its hanger and several things were pushed closely together.

Her heart pounding fiercely, she went to her door and listened after turning out her light. The rest of the house was quiet. The children had fallen to sleep almost immediately. The silent halls were empty, and no lights shone from the servants' wing.

Once, she thought she'd call Jeff. He'd made her promise she would if anything developed. She sat in the dark, trying to decide what to do. She sniffed the cigarette ashes. She didn't feel very brave, only frightened.

She couldn't tell Barrett now. It would be ridiculous to worry him. She wished that she and Jeff had gone right to the police.

Maybe her nephew Courtney had been in her room looking for something.

That was plain stupid! Courtney never came in without an invitation. Judith? Well, a little girl might be interested in her auntie's new clothes. Just a little sneak preview!

Charla climbed into her bed and plumped up her pillow. "Of course." She smiled in the dark. "Of course it was Judy!"

She was almost asleep when she heard the clock downstairs strike twelve. She suddenly sat up. "But Judy doesn't smoke cigarettes!"

At that instant a rough hand was suddenly clamped across her mouth. She tried to scream, but the sound gurgled in her throat and the sweet sickening smell of a drug penetrated her nostrils.

She sank into a black well . . .

When she regained consciousness she was sitting on a straight chair, in a bare room with only one very high window. She was tied securely to the chair.

A light was burning, although she could tell that it was probably early dawn, as a little light came through the old cracked blind at the window.

It might be a while yet before her people would even discover that she wasn't in her room back home, because sometimes she slept late on Saturday mornings. However, she remembered that Jeff was coming for her at ten, and she'd asked for a tray about nine, which someone would bring up. She always wore her watch, but the dial had been broken. She felt bruised, and she saw that her feet had been covered lightly with a small grey blanket. Her hands and ankles had been bound rather tightly, but the rest of the cords were a bit looser. The room was chilly and she wished she had a cup of coffee, although there was a brackish taste in her mouth.

She was shaking again, and she tried to be calm. She saw that her watch had stopped a few minutes after twelve. She wondered where she could possibly be. It could be almost anywhere! The floor was quite rough, needed cleaning, and one couldn't say if the room were in an old office building or in a house. She strained to hear any sound, but there seemed to be utter silence everywhere.

After a long time she dropped off into a doze, although she was very uncomfortable. She was awakened by the scraping of a key in the lock, and two masked men entered.

One carried a small tray of food, and even though she felt nauseated and horribly frightened, she was grateful that one was fairly considerate.

"Miss, we'll come right to the point. We know you took the bolt of cloth from the shipping box. Where is it?"

She stared at them. Yes, that was direct. And it was to the point. How could they possibly know? And how could it even have been missed? Had they planned to do something with it that very night?

She must not give anything away. They must not know that Jeff would be taking it to the police this morning. She wished she knew the time. If only he'd already gone.

"Where's the cloth, miss? Quit stalling for time."

"What cloth are you talking about? I work in a draper's shop where there are thousands of bolts of material that go through our store every season. What cloth are you talking about?"

"Ain't you the innocent? You know very well what we mean."

Maybe she could pretend ignorance. Maybe she would be able to convince them she knew nothing about it.

"Do you mean some red velvet that got mixed up with an order that went to South Africa by mistake last week?"

"No, indeed we don't! We mean the bolt of silk you've been so interested in. What's your interest in it, miss?"

"Oh, you mean that pretty blue cloth with the white flowers? I gave up the idea long ago. Just wanted to have a party dress made from it. Funniest thing, I never got my order in on time. I do hope they have it again next year."

"She's just real smart, isn't she? Don't

pretend with us, miss. It was in the shipping box, and now it's not. What happened to it?"

"Sometimes I think that silk isn't real. First someone sees it; then he doesn't. It just disappears."

"Drink your coffee, and we'll wait until you come to your senses. When you tell us where it is, we'll turn you loose. And if you don't tell us, we can make you talk, you know."

The taller man untied her hands. Her fingers were limp and she could hardly hold the cup to her lips. She forced a little of the colt biscuit down, and drank all of the coffee.

"Now, if you know what's good for you, you'll start talking."

Her lips trembling, she asked, "What time is it?"

"What does time matter? You won't be going anywhere." The shorter man spoke angrily. "Tell us what we want to know and we'll let you go."

"My folks will be worried by now, They'll go right to the police."

"They're being watched, too."

Sudden fear for Barrett and his family

shot through her. She hoped Jeff had been in touch with the police by now. They must have become aware of her disappearance and her room must surely show signs of a struggle.

"Where's the material, miss? We have to find out. We've gotten our orders. I hate to hurt a woman, though."

"Oh, stop acting like a gentleman and get on with it. I'll not mind hitting her."

"Please let me think about it a few minutes."

"No," said the shorter man. "You ain't going to get no more time. Start telling us what you done with the cloth or I'm going to start hitting you." He stepped menacingly toward her.

I'm not brave at all. I'm going to tell where it is, she thought as he slapped her across the cheek.

His hands left a vivid streak and the tears spurted silently from her eyes. The men retreated to the door and talked quietly. One of them left, and she was glad it was the impatient one.

As she sat waiting for she knew not what, she reviewed many details. Had

Mr. Craigie really gone hunting up in Scotland? Had someone been in the shipping room yesterday during the lunch and caught her snooping around that box? If so, why hadn't they watched it more closely and taken care of it before she and Jeff had removed it?

Late that afternoon both men left. She had had nothing more to eat, and was almost hysterical by the next morning when no one had returned. She pounded the walls, she tried to send her voice up to the closed window. She had managed to inch the chair over against the outer wall. She heard nothing but a train whistle and was confused about the number of times she had heard it.

She sank into a kind of rough-edged slumber after daybreak and was suddenly wakened by voices outside the door. Someone tried the door. Then the lock was shot off and she saw Jeff and a man in uniform, followed by other men.

"Oh, Jeff!" Charla cried weakly.

He had her cut loose in a moment and pulled her into his arms. He whispered many things to her, but the thing which he repeated oftenest, was, "Oh, Charla, Charla, my little love."

The next hour was blurred, and it was late that evening before she had the full story from Jeff.

"Diamond smugglers, dear. It's quite a fiction-like plot. Each season a special fabric was chosen, easily identifiable, such as the blue you unfortunately desired for a dress. The Scotland Yard men knew that something was going on, but they'd been unable to locate how these diamonds were being sent to America."

"Then someone at Martyns-Oblinskey in New York was cooperating?"

Jeff nodded. "Yes, and very well. The bolt of material has an inner packing core. It's fairly easy to conceal a packet of gems inside it, since no customs officer would be likely to search a legitimate routine shipment of fabrics to a dress manufacturer."

"Who's in it at the shop?" Charla really knew the answer.

"Craigie, of course, Mrs. Tomlinson, and that's really all. But your brother's gardener Mike is in on the deal. Of course, it's a big operation. There are five people caught up in the net right in London. Barrett's going to have to look for a new gardener."

"I made one mistake, Jeff. I didn't tell you about the cutting of the saddle strap on Vixen. I took a nasty spill, but didn't want to worry Barrett and Jennie by talking about it."

Jeff's face whitened. "When I think of all you've been let in for, and part of it my fault! We should have gone right to the police the night we took the material from the packing crate."

"I just don't see why Mike had to bother me with all of those near-accidents."

"Don't underestimate the extent to which he would have gone. He's wanted in several countries, stops at very little, is a sort of strong man. Once you were suspicious of things at the shop, the best thing was to get you out of the way. An accident looks good, and would have settled you once and for all."

Charla shivered. She had been very foolish. She should have discussed all of this with her brother months ago. If he hadn't been so thankful to have her back unharmed, he would most certainly have been very angry with her for keeping her fears a secret.

"In the meantime, I've been doing a little research on Craigie. He's the chief, and I've had a private detective watching him for some time. He wasn't on his way to Scotland, Charla. He was nabbed at Victoria Station, had two airlines tickets, one for Vienna, the other for Johannesburg. That would take care of his problems for a while at least."

"Barrett's going to need some help down at the shop."

"Yes, indeed. Some replacements. One for Craigie, one for Mrs. Tomlinson, and one for you."

Charla raised her brows. "I'm perfectly all right now. I can go right ahead with my work."

"Even though your career is going to be acting as wife to me?" Jeff kissed her tenderly.

She closed her eyes. He kissed her again.

"That would make a difference." she smiled. "Yes, I can see that Barrett will need to replace me, too."

THE END

CLOUD OVER MALVERTON
Nancy Buckingham

Dulcie soon realises that something is seriously wrong at Malverton, and when violence strikes she is horrified to find herself under suspicion of murder.

AFTER THOUGHTS
Max Bygraves

The Cockney entertainer tells stories of his East End childhood, of his RAF days, and his post-war showbusiness successes and friendships with fellow comedians.

MOONLIGHT
AND MARCH ROSES
D. Y. Cameron

Lynn's search to trace a missing girl takes her to Spain, where she meets Clive Hendon. While untangling the situation, she untangles her emotions and decides on her own future.

NURSE ALICE IN LOVE
Theresa Charles

Accepting the post of nurse to little Fernie Sherrod, Alice Everton could not guess at the romance, suspense and danger which lay ahead at the Sherrod's isolated estate.

POIROT INVESTIGATES
Agatha Christie

Two things bind these eleven stories together — the brilliance and uncanny skill of the diminutive Belgian detective, and the stupidity of his Watson-like partner, Captain Hastings.

LET LOOSE THE TIGERS
Josephine Cox

Queenie promised to find the long-lost son of the frail, elderly murderess, Hannah Jason. But her enquiries threatened to unlock the cage where crucial secrets had long been held captive.

THE TWILIGHT MAN
Frank Gruber

Jim Rand lives alone in the California desert awaiting death. Into his hermit existence comes a teenage girl who blows both his past and his brief future wide open.

DOG IN THE DARK
Gerald Hammond

Jim Cunningham breeds and trains gun dogs, and his antagonism towards the devotees of show spaniels earns him many enemies. So when one of them is found murdered, the police are on his doorstep within hours.

THE RED KNIGHT
Geoffrey Moxon

When he finds himself a pawn on the chessboard of international espionage with his family in constant danger, Guy Trent becomes embroiled in moves and countermoves which may mean life or death for Western scientists.

TIGER TIGER
Frank Ryan

A young man involved in drugs is found murdered. This is the first event which will draw Detective Inspector Sandy Woodings into a whirlpool of murder and deceit.

CAROLINE MINUSCULE
Andrew Taylor

Caroline Minuscule, a medieval script, is the first clue to the whereabouts of a cache of diamonds. The search becomes a deadly kind of fairy story in which several murders have an other-worldly quality.

LONG CHAIN OF DEATH
Sarah Wolf

During the Second World War four American teenagers from the same town join the Army together. Forty-two years later, the son of one of the soldiers realises that someone is systematically wiping out the families of the four men.

THE LISTERDALE MYSTERY
Agatha Christie

Twelve short stories ranging from the light-hearted to the macabre, diverse mysteries ingeniously and plausibly contrived and convincingly unravelled.

TO BE LOVED
Lynne Collins

Andrew married the woman he had always loved despite the knowledge that Sarah married him for reasons of her own. So much heartache could have been avoided if only he had known how vital it was to be loved.

ACCUSED NURSE
Jane Converse

Paula found herself accused of a crime which could cost her her job, her nurse's reputation, and even the man she loved, unless the truth came to light.

A GREAT DELIVERANCE
Elizabeth George

Into the web of old houses and secrets of Keldale Valley comes Scotland Yard Inspector Thomas Lynley and his assistant to solve a particularly savage murder.

'E' IS FOR EVIDENCE
Sue Grafton

Kinsey Millhone was bogged down on a warehouse fire claim. It came as something of a shock when she was accused of being on the take. She'd been set up. Now she had a new client — herself.

A FAMILY OUTING IN AFRICA
Charles Hampton and Janie Hampton

A tale of a young family's journey through Central Africa by bus, train, river boat, lorry, wooden bicycle and foot.

THE PLEASURES OF AGE
Robert Morley

The author, British stage and screen star, now eighty, is enjoying the pleasures of age. He has drawn on his experiences to write this witty, entertaining and informative book.

THE VINEGAR SEED
Maureen Peters

The first book in a trilogy which follows the exploits of two sisters who leave Ireland in 1861 to seek their fortune in England.

A VERY PAROCHIAL MURDER
John Wainwright

A mugging in the genteel seaside town turned to murder when the victim died. Then the body of a young tearaway is washed ashore and Detective Inspector Lyle is determined that a second killing will not go unpunished.

DEATH ON A
HOT SUMMER NIGHT
Anne Infante

Micky Douglas is either accident-prone or someone is trying to kill him. He finds himself caught in a desperate race to save his ex-wife and others from a ruthless gang.

HOLD DOWN A SHADOW
Geoffrey Jenkins

Maluti Rider, with the help of four of the world's most wanted men, is determined to destroy the Katse Dam and release a killer flood.

THAT NICE MISS SMITH
Nigel Morland

A reconstruction and reassessment of the trial in 1857 of Madeleine Smith, who was acquitted by a verdict of Not Proven of poisoning her lover, Emile L'Angelier.

SEASONS OF MY LIFE
Hannah Hauxwell
and Barry Cockcroft

The story of Hannah Hauxwell's struggle to survive on a desolate farm in the Yorkshire Dales with little money, no electricity and no running water.

TAKING OVER
Shirley Lowe and Angela Ince

A witty insight into what happens when women take over in the boardroom and their husbands take over chores, children and chickenpox.

AFTER MIDNIGHT STORIES,
The Fourth Book Of

A collection of sixteen of the best of today's ghost stories, all different in style and approach but all combining to give the reader that special midnight shiver.

DEATH TRAIN
Robert Byrne

The tale of a freight train out of control and leaking a paralytic nerve gas that turns America's West into a scene of chemical catastrophe in which whole towns are rendered helpless.

THE ADVENTURE OF THE CHRISTMAS PUDDING
Agatha Christie

In the introduction to this short story collection the author wrote "This book of Christmas fare may be described as 'The Chef's Selection'. I am the Chef!"

RETURN TO BALANDRA
Grace Driver

Returning to her Caribbean island home, Suzanne looks forward to being with her parents again, but most of all she longs to see Wim van Branden, a coffee planter she has known all her life.

SKINWALKERS
Tony Hillerman

The peace of the land between the sacred mountains is shattered by three murders. Is a 'skinwalker', one who has rejected the harmony of the Navajo way, the murderer?

A PARTICULAR PLACE
Mary Hocking

How is Michael Hoath, newly arrived vicar of St. Hilary's, to meet the demands of his flock and his strained marriage? Further complications follow when he falls hopelessly in love with a married parishioner.

A MATTER OF MISCHIEF
Evelyn Hood

A saga of the weaving folk in 18th century Scotland. Physician Gavin Knox was desperately seeking a cure for the pox that ravaged the slums of Glasgow and Paisley, but his adored wife, Margaret, stood in the way.

DEAD SPIT
Janet Edmonds

Government vet Linus Rintoul attempts to solve a mystery which plunges him into the esoteric world of pedigree dogs, murder and terrorism, and Crufts Dog Show proves to be far more exciting than he had bargained for . . .

A BARROW IN THE BROADWAY
Pamela Evans

Adopted by the Gordillo family, Rosie Goodson watched their business grow from a street barrow to a chain of supermarkets. But passion, bitterness and her unhappy marriage aliented her from them.

THE GOLD AND THE DROSS
Eleanor Farnes

Lorna found it hard to make ends meet for herself and her mother and then by chance she met two men — one a famous author and one a rich banker. But could she really expect to be happy with either man?

THE SONG OF THE PINES
Christina Green

Taken to a Greek island as substitute for David Nicholas's secretary, Annie quickly falls prey to the island's charms and to the charms of both Marcus, the Greek, and David himself.

GOODBYE DOCTOR GARLAND
Marjorie Harte

The story of a woman doctor who gave too much to her profession and almost lost her personal happiness.

DIGBY
Pamela Hill

Welcomed at courts throughout Europe, Kenelm Digby was the particular favourite of the Queen of France, who wanted him to be her lover, but the beautiful Venetia was the mainspring of his life.

Lott Betty
Walker
Richards
B. Powers
Frederick
Esther
Worthington
Bregg
Mom
Schumacher
LH

SEP   1995 WESTSIDE S.C.

Rdgsmh AL
Frederick
MAY   1996 EAST WYNDS

CSAL
FEB 97   B.S.C.
MAR 97   TRACYTON
MAR 98   CHARTER HOUSE

Sisman
Moore
Fritzler
9. a.